LONG RIDE TO LARAMIE

(BOOK 3)

MAKING TRACKS

GREG E JONES

ISBN: 1492359580
ISBN 13: 9781492359586

CHAPTER 1

FINALLY HOME (1877)

It would be a long ride to Laramie, and Amos was already tired. He was facing a two hundred mile trip and the first eighty miles would take him and his friends across the seemingly endless Red Desert to Wamsutter where they could catch the train.

The long summer they had spent at the Bear Paw and WIND Ranches, near Lander Wyoming figuring out the military connection to a rustling operation had been physically and mentally exhausting. Amos did not feel very much like talking. The memory of the senseless death of Joe Qualls, the Bear Paw Ranch foreman, was weighing heavily on his mind. These were the times that made him question what he was doing.

Fortunately they would get to stop in the railroad town of Carbon at one of the TIC Ranch houses for a few days before going on to Laramie. The huge TIC Ranch employed Amos as a cowboy and range detective. Amos and his friends, Riley and Jacob, had left the Bear Paw Ranch in midmorning and planned to travel about fifteen miles, then camp on upper Alkali Creek. From there it would be an easy day to Battle Springs and another easy day to Wamsutter.

By early afternoon they had reached the joining of Alkali Creek and the Sweetwater River. Amos asked his two friends to go on ahead up the creek and make camp while he visited the grave he had helped dig only a few days before. He laid a few rocks in the crude shape of a cross, then scratched Joe Qualls name on a flat rock and placed it at the head of the grave. He stood for a long time at the foot of the grave wishing he had words to say, but found none. He had been absently scratching his horse's ears and neck for well over an hour. The sun was sinking lower and it was time to head for camp.

"Daniel, my old friend," he said to his horse, "sometimes you have to let go, just to keep holding on." He turned to get in the saddle only to find Jacob and Riley standing silently behind him. "I thought you guys were going to make camp," he said.

"Some things are just more important," Riley said as he put his hand on Amos's shoulder. Riley O'Riley was his close friend, also a cowboy and sometimes range detective for the TIC Ranch.

"We can always make a camp," Jacob said as he looked at him with his almost black eyes. "It is not always possible to support your brother." He put his hand on Amos's other shoulder. Jacob Rides Horse Hanley was one of the last few Sheep Eater Indians that lived in the Medicine Bow Mountains. As a baby he had been "found" and adopted by white people. He was educated in the east, then in England, as a geologist. He still spoke with a slight British accent. He had returned to Wyoming where he had found his people. His Indian father had adopted both Riley and Amos as his sons. The three brothers, one Irish, one Indian and one that was a little bit of about everything, headed for camp.

That night they had the roast antelope and biscuits the cook from the Bear Paw Ranch had sent along, as well as beans and coffee. It was warm and Amos lay on his bed roll looking at the stars and thinking for several hours.

It turned cold over night and morning brought a strong cold breeze from the northwest. There were clouds hanging on the Wind River Mountains and November was trying to bring winter to Wyoming.

"We better stay moving," Riley said. "By the looks of the mountains we've only got about two days to make it to Wamsutter."

"I don't believe we are fortunate enough to have that much time," Jacob said, looking warily to the west. "It looks to me like we could be riding in a bit of snow by tomorrow."

"We've got about twenty five miles to make before we get to Battle Spring. We better keep moving along. There is just not a whole lot of firewood at Battle Spring," Amos said, sharing Jacob's apprehension.

In little more than five hours they had made it to the water tank left at the spring by mustangers. Their thoughts of having two days travel time had quickly been destroyed by the blizzard that rolled in behind them. It had looked like a dark rolling wave pursuing them across the flats.

As they let their horses drink, dollar sized snowflakes began blowing by in the wind. Jacob rummaged around in his saddlebags for a moment. "My brothers, we do not have much of a chance if we try to stay here tonight. In a short time we will not be able to see where we are going. Fortunately I have this, and can keep us headed south," he said holding up a compass. "Eventually we will come to the railroad tracks and can determine which way we should go from there."

"He's right," Riley hollered above the wind. "We better get whatever we have to stay warm with pulled on and get moving." Amos nodded in agreement.

"Take this just in case it gets real bad," Amos said as he took the rope from his saddle and handed one end to Riley. "Jacob, since you have the compass, you take the lead. Just let me have a rope between us," he said as he strung his rope over his pack-horse to Riley.

By midafternoon they could scarcely see the ground ahead of them. Fortunately it was not extremely cold, but at just below freezing the conditions were perfect for heavy snow. They still had over ten miles to go, and they were not sure just where they were going. As the storm rolled in, the long grey evening light that accompanies a high desert snowstorm began to turn black. Amos could feel fatigue setting in to himself and his horse, and the shoulder that had been injured near Centennial was aching. He half dozed in the saddle and tried to catch himself, knowing full well that falling asleep in these conditions could very easily bring death.

It was well into darkness when he jerked his head up for the umpteenth time. He saw two large trees on either side of him, the wind was howling through them. He yelled at Jacob to stop. The three of them came close together and Amos yelled, "Maybe we should think about trying to camp in this bunch of trees."

"I don't remember there being any trees out here," Riley said trying to shake the cobwebs out of his head. "Have we gone way too far south?"

Jacob must have nodded off too. He looked around for a minute trying to make sense of it. "Gentlemen, these are not trees, they are the pilings of a railroad bridge," he yelled. "That is not the wind roaring, it is the train going by!"

"We've got to stop it then!" Riley started to turn his horse.

"We can't stop it." Amos sounded dejected.

"Quickly," Jacob yelled over the rumbling. "What time is it?"

Amos dug for his pocket watch. "About ten minutes to seven," he shouted. "What the hell difference does it make?" The rumbling had faded.

"Because the train gets to Wamsutter at seven and takes an hour to take on fuel and water and change crews!" Jacob yelled excitedly. "If your watch and the train are both on time, then Wamsutter is a couple of miles west of here! All we have to do is follow the tracks and we should come right into town!"

"My watch says the same thing," Riley yelled back. "Let's get going!"

The heavy wet snow was almost a foot deep and the ground underneath was slippery. However, the horses had rested for a few minutes and were ready to go again. Jacob led the way from under the bridge and onto the tracks. Fortunately the train had blown the snow off and the horses had a nearly bare track bed to travel on. The wind was now almost straight into them and snow stuck to their faces. They moved along quickly and in thirty minutes almost ran into the back of the train that was still stopped at the Wamsutter depot. They made their way to the livery stable. There was no one there, but there was open stall space and they put their horses away, making sure they had extra feed and water. Amos left his bandanna on while the snow melted from his face and Riley did the same. Only Jacob seemed to be unaffected by the driving snow.

They left five dollars and a note where the owner could easily find it, then went to the boarding house. It was late, but the boarding house was still open to take care of any of the train crew that might be changing shifts. There was even a hot hearty supper and hot coffee. Only one room was available, but as tired as they were a pad on the floor and all the blankets they could find were more than enough. They were asleep in minutes.

They did not rise early the next morning. Amos had been awake for nearly two hours before he decided it was time to get out of his nice warm bed. Finally the smell of bacon frying and hot coffee was more than he could stand. The three had left their wet clothes hanging and they were pretty well dried, except for their boots. These they left at the bottom of the door where a draft of warm air was coming up from below. They went downstairs in their stocking feet to have breakfast.

Breakfast was bacon, eggs, biscuits and gravy and most importantly lots of hot coffee. The water in Wamsutter is a little alkaline to say the least, and the taste came through in the coffee. However, it was still good enough not to be wasted. Amos had a second and even a third cup. Breakfast had started at seven o'clock that morning and Amos had just finished his coffee at eight. The three of them finally went back upstairs, pulled on almost dry boots and got their gear. Riley went to book passage on the train that would be in at nine that morning. Meanwhile, Amos and Jacob went to the livery stable to saddle and pack the horses and square up with the blacksmith.

The livery stable owner was a jovial block of a man that looked to be as wide as he was tall. Amos thought he looked remarkably like a shorter version of Mac MacTavish, the farrier in Rock River. Indeed he was another Scot named Angus Clark, and he knew Mac MacTavish of Rock River and Tom Sherman Senior and Junior of Medicine Bow and Laramie. It seemed that there was a brotherhood between blacksmiths, just as there was between cowboys, miners and just about any other hardworking people.

"If ye managed to cross the Red Desert in one day in that snowstorm," Clark said and laughed, "then I can say that I have truly met the luckiest people in the world. I have also met three crazy people, all at the same time."

"Sometimes it's better to be lucky than good," Amos said as he smiled. "If the Lord watches out for children and fools, then he certainly has his hands full with the three of us." They had finished saddling the horses and packing up when they heard the train whistle. They headed for the door leading the horses.

"By the way lads, I did nay catch your names," the farrier said.

"Sorry, I didn't mean to be rude," Amos said. "This is Jacob Rides Horse Hanley," he said as he motioned toward Jacob. "And I'm Amos Moss." He extended his hand.

"You're Amos Moss then?" Clark said as they shook hands. "There were a couple of soldiers in here looking for ye a while back. Aire ye the same fella?"

"Yeah, I probably am," Amos said with a chuckle. "Whatever became of them?"

"Well, they spent a few days sitting around watching the train come in, and depleting the local whiskey supply, before they gave up and left." Clark chuckled. "They did nay have a lot of kind words to say about ye. Especially the day they spent looking for their horses." He chuckled again. "Did they ever catch up to ye?"

"Yeah, we got all squared up a week or so ago," Amos said shrugging his shoulders. "They probably won't be coming back this way for a while."

They led the horses to the train where they met Riley. It took a few minutes to get enough of the snow off of a loading ramp to safely load their animals. Then they headed to the nearest passenger car. In warmer weather they would've ridden with the horses, but they were still tired enough not to want to get chilled again. The horses were still tired enough that they would just stand still for the ride.

The snow lay over a foot deep on the level. Of course, with the wind there was no such thing as level. Even so, the storm was passing and only occasional swirling showers of snow blew by. The temperature hovered just above freezing and patches of blue sky could be seen to the east. The train pulled out and a short time later stopped at Rawlins where there was about half as much snow.

Amos took a few minutes to find Bill Mount, the cow puncher at the stockyards. He quickly told him about the events of the last few months and the death of Corporal Lewis, or whoever he might be.

"Well, I guess there won't be much need to kick his ass now," Bill said. "It's too bad he had to die for a bunch of cows. I guess I'm glad to know that it wasn't my fault that rustled cattle were getting shipped out of here."

"I never thought it was, Bill," Amos said as he extended his hand and then headed for the door. He went back to the train and got on board a few minutes before it left for Fort Steele.

Amos considered going to the officers' quarters to talk to Sergeant Harrison and the fort's commander, Colonel Stankowski. However, soldiers don't tend to be friendly towards people who get their own killed and the events of the last weeks might be thought of that way by some soldiers. Between the three of them they decided it would be better to wait for a while until things had calmed down and the truth of the situation had sunk in. They stayed on the train, only going out to check on their horses.

The sun was headed for the western horizon when they finally got to the Carbon train station. One of the three TIC Ranch houses was on a hill overlooking the railroad town of Carbon. From there the lower workings of the ranch were overseen. A second house was in the upper reaches of the Medicine Bow River and oversaw the high country workings of the ranch. The third house was actually in the town of Medicine Bow and oversaw the shipping of cattle and supplies, as well as the overall management and bookkeeping. A forth house was under construction near the old stage crossing at Elk Mountain.

The storm that had nearly been their undoing in the Red Desert had left barely an inch of snow at Carbon. Most of that had melted so that only a small amount of snow still lay in the shaded areas. It had been a beautiful warm day when they'd left what now seemed like years ago. Now, with winter coming on, the place seemed almost unfamiliar. They unloaded their mounts and rode up to the ranch house. The horses were taken care of and their gear put in the bunkhouse. As they walked into the dining hall in the main house, old Charlie the cook was just pouring three cups of coffee. Each cup sat next to a bowl of his fruit upside-down cake. "Welcome back boys," he said as he pointed to the coffee. They were finally home.

CHAPTER 2

A BIT OF GRAIN (1877)

Winter had taken a swing at Amos and his friends and had barely missed. The patch on his face and Riley's, where their bandanas had stuck, turned out to be mild frost bite. Two days after they got to Carbon the healing process started and with it came interminable itch. Only Jacob was unaffected and showed no signs of the ordeal. To add insult to injury the weather had turned warm again and a beautiful late fall was in progress. The roundup was over and some of the cowboys were having a leisurely breakfast.

Over coffee Riley asked Jacob why he was not suffering. "I attribute it to the supernatural strength of my Indian heritage," he said as he poked a finger skyward and tried not to smile. "And the fact that my bandana was made by my people. It has two layers of soft rabbit hide with the fur layered between them. I believe I now know what to get you two for Christmas."

"You snuck up on me again," Amos said as he and Riley both scowled. "Didn't ya? Well, tell me then, 'Doctor D'Artagnan', how long are we going to have to suffer to satisfy your sense of humor this time?" Amos referred to an earlier incident when Riley had claimed Jacob was a French doctor in order to save the life of a man who hated Indians. Among other things, Jacob spoke fluent French.

"Actually, I do want to apologize for that," Jacob said looking at them. "I did not realize your plight until we were unsaddling the horses and by then it was too late."

"Well, it's not your fault that we were too dumb to figure it out," Riley said. "What have you got in that magic bag of yours to slow down this damn itch?"

"In fact," Jacob said with relief, "I did make up something that should help." He pulled a small jar from his pocket. "This is petroleum grease with a small amount of powdered willow bark painkiller mixed in. A light coat is all you need, and do not scratch or rub at it. You should be healed in a week or two, but the affected area will be sensitive for the rest of the winter. Keep it covered when you're out in the cold."

"Speaking of out in the cold," Shamus Clancy, the foreman of the Carbon Ranch, said as he walked in and set his usual half cup of mostly cold coffee on the table. "That's where I should send you three after you missed our roundup and went on one for another ranch," he said and laughed. "Actually Ted Brow tells me that he met with the Federal Marshall and the amount of money that will be coming back here is way more than we would've paid all three of you in several years." He laughed again. "It's been decided that the ranch makes more money when you're not here than when you are, so they are going to fire all of you."

Several of the men looked around, as Riley looked into his coffee cup and said very seriously, "See Amos, there is a God." Everyone in the room broke into laughter. Charlie the cook came out of the kitchen to see what all the fuss was about, and brought a pot of coffee with him.

"Riley, you crazy son of a bitch," Clancy said as he was trying to wipe up the coffee he had splashed out of his cup. Charlie refilled his cup and grinned as he threw him a damp rag. "I forgot how peaceful it is here when you three are gone." Clancy laughed again. "Okay, if you can be serious for a minute, I've got some things to tell you. First, they took Major Tibbs to Fort Sanders to stand court-martial and you're going to have to testify at his trial. Next, Mister Cullen has pulled a few strings and you're going to get paid a percentage of the value of the cattle that were recovered as well as the money that will be repaid to the other ranchers that lost cattle. Then, Marshall Hanley wants to talk to you about being part of some sort of posse that's trying to run down a gang of horse thieves. Finally, a friend of Mister Cullen, from over near Laramie Peak, has been losing cows in some strange way and has asked to have you look into it. Everyone is supposed to be in Laramie in mid-December to meet with Mister Cullen and that includes you three."

Timothy Ivanovich Cullen's family had come to America as dirt-poor Irish immigrants. He had risen from nothing to own the TIC ranch, a part of the railroad, several mining interests, the bank in Laramie and those were just his Wyoming holdings. He had become a powerful man and he had taken a liking to Amos, Jacob and Riley. Most of his cowboys were poor Scots and Irish kids from immigrant families that had pooled their money to get Cullen started. He was making those families wealthy. He valued trust and loyalty above all other things and was as generous to those who gave it to him as he was vicious with those who betrayed him or stole from him.

"Why are they taking him to Fort Sanders?" Amos asked.

"From what I can gather," Clancy said, "they want the trial to be in Albany County because they think he is more likely to be safe and get a fair trial there. A number of officers and enlisted men were affected in the other two forts, but no one was hurt in Fort Sanders. Plus, the Cattlemen's Association requested that the trial be held in Laramie, and they're starting to have quite a bit of clout."

"That certainly makes it easier for us," Jacob said. "In the meantime I need to make certain my people have adequate food supplies. With your permission, I will ride over there and try to procure some sort of meat for them."

"Yeah, I'd like you to do that," Clancy said. He was serious again. "We took some stuff to them a few weeks ago, but I'd like you to go on over just in case the winter sets in cold again. And take these two 'Wind River Cowboys', heavy on the wind, with you. They've probably forgotten their way around here already." He chuckled. "By the way, a little herd of buffalo was spotted over that way a couple of days ago, so you might want to take a wagon. We got another wagon while you were gone, so you might as well use it." He rose and went back to his office.

"Well, one of the wagons is here," Riley said as he gulped his last swallow of coffee. "I'll go get it hitched up and you guys get some gear together. We'll be to the upper place this evening. Don't forget salt and dried apples."

Jacob and Amos rounded up the necessary supplies, including bedrolls and heavy bullet cartridges for the Sharps rifles. They were on their way in half an hour. It was a beautiful November day. There was sharpness in the air but the temperature was fairly warm. Even so, Amos and Riley wore bandannas around their faces because of the frostbite. The aspen had changed colors and the smell of wet leaves and sage was in the air. The sun was on the horizon when they got to the Upper River Ranch house.

They went into the barn to take care of the horses. The team was unhitched and they were just putting their saddles on saddle trees when someone drew back the hammer on a pistol. Amos started to reach for his Schofield but a voice behind him said, "Don't try it Mister! Just get your hands in the air!" It was hard to mistake Ian MacGill's voice. Amos's hands were still halfway up when he turned around.

"Are you related to that sneaky son of a bitch?" he asked as he motioned towards Jacob, who was grinning broadly.

"I keep promising to teach you to listen like an Indian," Jacob said chuckling. "If you had you would have heard him when he came out of the house." He paused for a moment. "I believe you can put your hands down now Mister O'Riley."

Riley's hands were still in the air and he smiled sheepishly as he lowered them. "You're right, Amos," he said with a grin. "You should have shot him when you had the chance."

"So why did you think it was necessary to scare the hell out of me and Riley?" Amos asked with mock aggravation.

Ian MacGill was the foreman of the Upper River Ranch portion of the TIC. He tried not to smirk. "Well, if you saw an Indian and two guys with bandannas around their faces sneak into your barn what would you do?" he asked.

"You knew darn well who we were! And we didn't exactly sneak in!" Riley sounded exasperated as he pulled the bandanna away. "We'd be pretty poor thieves to come sneaking in here and leave our horses and all our gear."

"Maybe you're just not too smart, as thieves go," MacGill said sarcastically, trying not to laugh. "Besides, I haven't seen you three in a long time. I guess I just didn't recognize you." He broke into a laugh, then extended his hand. "Welcome home boys, come on in. Cookie has supper just about ready."

All was forgiven until they got inside the main house and discovered that everyone inside had been watching. They quickly became the butt of a number of good natured jokes. Even the cook got in on it.

"Coffee, Amos?" he asked. "You don't have to hold up both hands, just the one with the cup in it." He chuckled as he poured good coffee. There was no point in trying to counter the jokes. They just let them play out for the rest of the evening.

After everyone had eaten, MacGill came over. He held both hands up as he sat down; Amos and Riley just scowled. "I assume you're going to want to take some supplies over to White Rocks," he said. "There are a few buffalo between here and there, up along the timber. We got a couple for ranch meat two days ago. I'm going to send a couple of the boys with you to help load the wagon. Once you get the meat there they can bring the wagon back, and you can spend however much time you want with Jacob's family."

It was a very good offer and the three men thanked MacGill. The next morning they headed out and, just as promised, there were about a dozen buffalo halfway to the White Rocks. Amos dropped two of them quickly and within an hour they were cleaned and loaded on the wagon. In another two hours they were unloading. Jacob's family had been at the White Rock cliffs that were their winter quarters for over two months and they were very glad to see Jacob and his adopted brothers again. The greeting ceremony was performed by a cousin who was the eldest son of Jacob's uncle.

"Something isn't right," Amos he said as he looked at the little group of Indians. "Our uncle isn't here."

"He has gone to be with his Mother the Mountain," Jacob said slowly through his tears. "We apparently missed him by only a few days."

Riley looked at the ground and said, "I really wish I could have heard his stories." He and Amos quickly went out to help carry another quarter of the buffalo into the overhang.

The younger man, who was apparently now considered to be the chief, came over to them. He took each of them by the right hand and held it in his left hand. He placed a yellow bead in their palms and closed their fingers around it. He then spoke a few words and went back to working on the buffalo.

"Another spirit watches over us," Amos said as he took the small memory pouch from around his neck and put the bead in it.

"How did you know what he said?" Jacob asked as he looked very questioningly at Amos.

"I guess you just get to know your people," Amos whispered as he went outside to stare at the sky for a moment while his tears dried.

The two ranch hands that had helped them took the wagon and headed back to the ranch house. Inside the overhang the smell of roasting ribs and stewing apples filled the air. The meal was plain, very filling and satisfying. The Indians were happy to receive the apples and the five pounds of salt that Amos and Riley always brought. The young man, who was now Chief, tried very hard to relate the stories that had been told by his father. Somehow, for Amos, the fullness and passion that had been told by the old Chief who had first adopted him just wasn't there in the younger man. He seemed to know that his people were not far from vanishing from the Earth.

They spent two days with the Sheep Eaters, then headed back to the ranch. It was a short side trip to the junction of Wagonhound Creek and the Medicine Bow River. It was the first opportunity Amos had to visit the grave of Bay, the first real horse he had ever had, and the horse that had brought him to Wyoming.

Amos stood for some time at the foot of the grave. He lowered the bandanna and held his hat in his hand. For some time he told the stories of the times they'd had together, then he spoke of his new horse, Daniel. When he had nothing left to tell he took a small amount of the sweetened grain he always kept in his pocket and sprinkled it over the grave. When he turned to ride away he saw Riley and Jacob standing with their hats in their hands a few yards away.

CHAPTER 3

DONE DEAL (1877)

A mos took a long time to write a letter to James Qualls, telling him of the death of his brother Joe, and of the funds that had been left to him. He placed emphasis on the opening that might be available with the Bear Paw Ranch.

There was little to do now but wait for the trial. December came along as it usually did; cold, windy and with short days. Thankfully there had not been a lot of snow. Riley, Amos and Jacob caught the train at Carbon along with the ranch foremen and were joined in Medicine Bow by Ted Brow, the overall TIC Ranch manager and bookkeeper. As they rode toward Rock River, Brow explained to them that the ranch had enjoyed a very good year. The money the ranch would receive for the recovered cows, along with that year's profits and additional money from Timothy Ivanovich Cullen was going to be used to buy the WIND Ranch and the Bear Paw Ranch. Furthermore, because of the recommendations made by Amos, Riley and United States Marshall Sam Hanley, Joe Qualls brother James was going to be interviewed for the job of manager of the Bear Paw Ranch.

Brow, who was usually serious about everything, laughed and said, "We might as well buy those two ranches; after all, half the cows up there belong to us or the SY anyway." The SY was owned by the Russian members of Cullen's family. "Besides that, you guys already know the way there and back," he chuckled then looked out the window. "Would you guys have anyone in mind to manage the WIND Ranch?" he asked.

"Pete and Al," Amos said without hesitation. "The Ivanovich boys." Riley was nodding his head. The Ivanovich cousins had helped Amos and Riley figure out that the rustled cattle from several ranches had ended up on the Indian Reservation at Fort Washakie.

"That didn't take too long," Brow said. "Tim agrees with you; he'll probably put Pete in charge of the cattle, and Al as business manager of both places. At least we would have someone whose honesty is not questionable."

The train stopped briefly in Rock River and Amos had a strong desire to stay there and visit his friends the MacTavishs. However, the trial was just two days away and it was probable that the attorneys would want to speak to him. In the back of his mind he decided that he would spend Christmas or New Year's with the big blacksmith. Two hours later they were at the depot in Laramie. Rooms had already been reserved at the hotel. Amos had not seen his good friend Sheriff Nathan Tower for almost a year. He was anxious to see how the new baby was coming along. After stowing his gear in his room he went to the Sheriff's office, only to find that Nathan was at Fort Sanders talking with the Post Commander. Rather than sit around waiting, the three decided to visit Tom Sherman Senior at the livery stable.

They arrived to find Tom Senior watching Olaf Nordquist, who had helped Amos with the de Mortimer case, putting shoes on a pair of draft horses. The job was about half done and Tom Senior seemed to approve. When he saw Amos come through the door he was delighted and shook hands with all three men. Amos had worked for Mister Sherman when he first came to Laramie.

"Come on back to my office," he said cheerfully. "Let me pour you a drink." They followed him to the little back room that served as an office. He put an extra lump of coal in the small stove, then set out glasses and poured a small shot for each of them. "I haven't seen you boys since last Christmas," he said. "Where have you been keeping yourselves?"

They filled him in on the events of the past summer, leaving out only the part about having to testify at the court-martial. When the story was finished Amos asked, "How is Olaf doing, and did they have a baby?" Olaf had met his wife Brandi at Lil's Sporting House, where she still worked.

"He's doing fine and they sure did." Tom Senior laughed and shrugged his shoulders. "It looks just like him too; black hair, real dark eyes, a little round face and he's a chunky little guy. "

"As I recall," Jacob said as he raised an eyebrow, "Mister and Missus Nordquist are tall, thin and have light hair."

"That's what I said," Tom Senior said and began to laugh. "The little fella looks just like him. They have another one on the way and I can't wait to see what this one looks like."

"Mister O'Riley," Jacob said seriously, "you seem to be rather relieved. I assume that is from your concern for the happy couple." Everyone had started laughing just as Olaf Nordquist came in.

"Dem horses is finished Mister Sherman," Olaf said as he looked in, smiling at everyone. "It is sure good to see you fellas again." He shook hands with everyone. "My vife and I haf a new baby boy," he said proudly.

"Yes," Riley said grinning. "Mr. Sherman here told us all about it. By the way, what did you name him?"

"Vell, ve haf named him Olaf Riley Nordquist," Olaf said through a wide grin. "My vife says she has always liked dat name."

Riley was sputtering and trying to say something. Amos was against the wall laughing and Jacob left the room. Olaf was quite confused. "Is der someting wrong?" he asked.

"No, Olaf, it's a wonderful name," Amos said as he tried to compose himself. "It just struck me funny how speechless Riley is to know that you named your baby after a cowhand."

"Oh, it's not like dat," Olaf said. "My vife yust likes dat name. It has noting to do vit dis Riley."

"No, I'm sure it doesn't," Amos said. "It just struck me funny. We wish you both all the happiness in the world."

"Vat about Mister Yacob?" Olaf asked. "Did I say someting wrong?"

"Not at all," Amos said. "Sometimes he gets emotional about these things." Amos was doing the best acting job of his life. "I'm sure Jacob went to say an Indian blessing for the baby."

Mister Sherman had been biting his lip. "Come on Olaf and let me check out your work," he said as he led his apprentice out the door. "Come back in the morning when we aren't as busy, boys," he said, looking over his shoulder and rolling his eyes.

Riley was still sputtering. "Come on, Daddy," Amos said as he grabbed Riley by the arm. "Let's get out of here before 'my vife' shows up and wants to name the next kid Rileyette."

They made it out the door to find Jacob leaning against the wall still laughing. "It's not that funny," Riley complained. His face was getting very red.

"Oh, Mister O'Riley, it is indeed that funny," Jacob said as he started laughing again. "Amos, I believe we should go out of our way to keep Mister O'Riley as far as possible from Lil's Sporting House, lest the Nordquist's have twins." Riley was scowling and Amos had joined Jacob leaning against the wall and laughing.

Riley was getting more frustrated. "That's not how it works anyway!" His voice was rising.

"Maybe not," Amos said as he slid down the wall laughing. "But I wouldn't put anything past you, Daddy."

Jacob had fallen to his hands and knees laughing. "You should see your face!" he laughed and pointed weakly at Riley. "I formerly thought your hair was red!" He started laughing again.

After a few minutes the laughter died down. "Jacob," Amos said as he laughed, "if you're done praying down there." Amos laid his arm across Riley's shoulder. "Let's get going. After supper I want to buy you a drink. I haven't had that good of a laugh in quite a while." The three brothers walked arm over shoulder toward the restaurant.

Riley and Jacob went on ahead while Amos went to the Sheriff's office to try to find Nathan. Fortunately he and his deputy were there. Since nothing much was going on Nathan left the office to his deputy and joined Amos. On the way Amos filled his friend in on the events of the previous few months and especially on the events of the afternoon.

All was peaceful and cheerful through the meal as the friends caught up on what had been going on. Nathan was obviously very proud of his new daughter and most of his conversation revolved around her and his wife Mary Beth. As the meal ended, Elbert

Richards the restaurant owner and Mary Beth's father came out to join the four. He brought coffee and Amos never wasted good coffee. This was exceptional and he was into his fourth cup. Elbert wasted no time in inviting everyone to Christmas dinner. It was not scheduled to be as big as it had been the year before, being only for family, but godfathers were considered to be family.

When the meal had settled for a while, they decided to have the promised after dinner drink. It was midweek and the saloon was not crowded. They found a table in the back corner of the room. As was their habit, Nathan and Amos sat with their backs to the wall. They'd had one drink and were slowly sipping a second when Nathan stood up. He held his glass up and said, "A toast, my friends, to family and children." They all stood and raised their glasses and were about to tap them together when Nathan said in a loud voice, "Congratulations Riley, it's a boy!"

It took a moment to sink in; then Riley sat straight down and hung his head. Amos and Jacob started laughing as Nathan stood, with his glass still high in the air, looking as stoic as he could. Riley swallowed the drink he had and poured another. "Am I ever going to hear the end of this?" he asked mournfully. He tried to sound as sorrowful as he could.

"My dear brother," Jacob said as seriously as he could, "that will depend on the upcoming blessed event and whether the birth is multiple or not. In any event, here's to you." Jacob took a sip from his glass. "You rascal." The laughter started again.

The four friends laughed and generally enjoyed each other's company for two more hours. Then it was time for Nathan to go by his office and then home. Riley had been the subject of a good number of jokes, but they all knew it was in fun and that each of them would get their turn.

The next morning the four men again met for breakfast, then rented a buggy and went to Fort Sanders. There were military attorneys for both sides as well as civilian attorneys representing the Federal Government, Willis Crane and the Indian agent. It had been decided that all matters pertaining to the case would be settled at one time. The military tribunal consisted of five high-ranking officers, while the civil matters would be handled by Judge Corbett from Denver. Since Amos, Jacob and Riley were important witnesses they were sequestered and allowed to speak only to the assorted officers and the judge. They were told to tell only the truth as precisely as they could. No attorneys were allowed to see them since they might try to influence them.

The first day dealt only with the military matters. Proof gathered by Jacob's adoptive cousin United States Marshall Samuel Craft Hanley, alias Sam Croft, along with Colonel Stankowski, the Commander of Fort Steele, showed that the real Corporal Martin Lewis was indeed deceased. The man who was using his identity was the now deceased Hiram Cohen, a member of an east coast crime family. Hanley gave proof that Cohen had been involved in numerous operations to defraud the military as well as rustling both horses and cattle from the area ranches. He felt that Tibbs, the former Fort Steele Commander, had been little more than a pawn in the whole thing. Because of Hanley's testimony Colonel Tibbs was allowed to plead guilty to the lesser charge of receiving funds from stolen property belonging to the Army. His overall record had been good and, since he was very close to retirement anyway, the panel decided to demote him to the rank of Captain and accept his immediate resignation and retirement. Several troopers who had been involved with transporting and driving the rustled cattle were given short prison terms and dishonorable discharges. The panel had thought to review the death of Corporal Martin Lewis, alias Hiram Cohen, but since it was shown that Cohen was actually a civilian, the matter was left to the civilian judge.

It had been a long day for Amos. The long hours of sitting and the stress of testifying had left him exhausted. He feared the next day would be worse.

Judge Corbett had reviewed the findings of the military tribunal and dismissed any charges dealing with the death of Cohen since horse theft was a hanging offense anyway and being killed twice seemed like a waste of effort. On the charge of aiding and abetting rustling, Willis Crane, owner of the WIND Ranch, was given one month in prison for each cow shown to have been rustled in the ledgers presented by Marshall Hanley. It was obvious that the Judge Corbett had no sense of humor about rustling and that Crane would spend several lifetimes in prison. The Indian agent at Fort Washakie was given ten years in prison with loss of all of his possessions as partial repayment for the damages.

When the disposition of the ranches was brought to question Ted Brow asked to speak. "Your Honor," he began, "I am at liberty to state that I have at my disposal enough funds to cover any and all losses listed in Marshall Hanley's ledgers. Further, I can state that the ranch that lost the largest percentage of cattle is in complete agreement with the purchase of the ranches in question. There is no money owing on the WIND Ranch but there is some due on the Bear Paw Ranch. That will be paid in full immediately. Finally, I can say that very capable management has been found for both ranches and they will be up and running this spring. In the meantime, the men working there will be kept on if they desire to be. With the court's permission the necessary transactions will be completed before the first of the year."

"I would like to know where you got the money to complete all these transactions," Judge Corbett said as he peered over his spectacles at Ted Brow.

Timothy Ivanovich Cullen stood up in the back of the room. "The money would come from me," he said. The deal was done.

CHAPTER 4

THREE SONS (1878)

Amos was very relieved to have the trial over. Although his testimony had taken only fifteen minutes, and had corroborated that of Marshall Hanley, it felt like he had been in front of the court for hours. Riley felt the same way, and only Jacob seemed to be unfazed.

"It was not unlike any oral exam from my days at the universities," he said flatly. "All I had to do was tell them that I gave documents to Marshall Hanley, and confirm what they said. If anyone has had a difficult time, it would be 'daddy'…"

"Don't you start that again!" Riley said loudly and pointed a finger at Jacob. "It dawned on me last night that Tom Sherman said that the baby has dark hair and dark eyes, and there's just one of the three of us who can say that." Riley pulled off his hat and shook his bright red hair.

Jacob had been caught off guard. "Well…she's…I mean!" he sputtered. "Oh damn." It was one of the few times Amos had heard Jacob use profanity. They had started laughing again when Timothy Cullen and Ted Brow came walking out.

"Why don't you let me in on this?" Cullen asked as he tipped his hat back and raised his eyebrows. "After these past few days I could use a good laugh too."

"Well, Sir," Amos began. "It has to do with the baby that Jacob and Riley have had together."

Both Brow and Cullen pushed their heads back and looked very questioningly at Jacob and Riley, who were both shaking their heads and trying to say no. Amos was laughing as he gave a full explanation that stopped the questioning looks but not the laughter.

"Boys, that's the best laugh I've had in months," Cullen said as he and Brow turned to leave. "I want you to meet me for supper. We have a number of things to talk about."

The good laugh had done wonders to relieve the stress of the day. The three men took their time to get to the restaurant. It was before five o'clock, but on the high plains that meant the December sun had already set. The shortest day of the year was quickly approaching. Amos hated the short days, but the winter solstice marked the turnaround toward spring and soon the days would get longer, an event that Amos had long considered to be his Christmas present. Even so, it would be a couple of months before it started to get warmer. They went into the restaurant and found that Brow, Cullen and Marshall Hanley had just arrived. A table in a back room had been set aside for them and places were set with the "good" plates and silverware. Cullen sat at the head of the table and motioned Amos to sit near him. "I want to make sure you understand everything I say," Cullen said. "Some of this is going to be quite important."

It was an excellent meal. Afterwards Cullen passed out cigars and poured an after dinner drink of very fine Irish rye whiskey. When a sip had been taken, and the cigars had been lit, he set his glass down and became serious.

"Gentlemen," he said as he looked around the table, "I have to tell you how pleased I am with the outcome of the events at Fort Washakie. That however is done, and a matter of some pressing urgency has arisen. There is a horse thief," Cullen chuckled, "who Captain Tibbs assures me is closely related to our Riley, doing business in this area. His name is James Middleton Riley, but he generally goes by Doc Middleton. Marshall Hanley will give you the necessary details. I have been made aware that the Wyoming Stock Growers Association will be forming a posse to be under the direction of Detective Bill Lykins, and will be working in association with the Union Pacific Railroad and a Department of Justice

Special Agent. The Marshall here will be part of that group. Since he has worked with you, and feels that you are very competent, he has asked that you be allowed to work with him in pursuing Middleton," Cullen said as he looked around the room. "I have no objection to this since it will probably benefit the TIC Ranch and several other concerns with which I'm involved. Middleton is a violent man; he murdered a man in Texas but managed to escape from prison. Then he was captured in Nebraska, but stabbed a soldier and escaped again. He has now come to Wyoming. With this in mind, I am not ordering you to go along. That will be totally your decisions, and I think you should take some time to think about it."

The room was quiet. Jacob rose to address the room. "I do not consider myself to be in the same law enforcement league as the other gentleman in this room," he said. "Nor do I consider myself to be as capable with firearms as these men. I am, first and foremost, a geologist, and as such I am employed in part by the mining company and in part by the railroad and I have primary obligations to those companies. My abilities in my chosen field are probably of much greater value to them, and the TIC ranch, than are my abilities as a range detective." He looked around the room. "This does not mean that I will not be available should it be necessary." He sat down.

"I completely respect that, Jacob. In fact, that is what I hoped you would say," Cullen said. "Riley, Amos, I want you to think about this for a while. If you decide to join the posse, Marshall Hanley will make sure that you are suitably paid. If you decide not to, then our deal at the ranch remains completely unchanged." The two men nodded.

"I hoped so also," Marshall Hanley said looking at Jacob. "I do appreciate that you will be available to give your opinion and your insight on whatever events might transpire during this action." Jacob nodded. The Marshall continued, "I forgot to mention that this operation will probably not take place until mid or late summer. So you probably have plenty of time to do anything else that needs to get done in the meantime."

"And that reminds me," Cullen said, looking at the last few drops of his drink. "An old friend of mine, who has a ranch up by

Laramie Peak, seems to be losing a few cows in a rather peculiar way. He asked me if I knew anyone who could do the detective work and I immediately thought of you three. If you wouldn't mind taking a trip up there this spring I'm sure he would be grateful, as would I." The three men nodded.

Christmas came along and Amos and his friends spent Christmas Eve with Nathan Tower and his family. On Christmas Day Cullen had a fantastic meal catered. Unbeknownst to anyone except Elbert Richards and his daughter, he'd had several train cars complete with cooking facilities and several chefs, as well as two dining cars, brought in the day before Christmas. Everyone who was family, friends, or just needed a meal was welcome. After everyone had eaten, Cullen stood at the front of the car and raised his glass. "This year has been particularly good to me and to my investors, due in no small part to a number of people in this car. It would be easy to thank the men who so greatly decreased rustling and horse thievery, but I also need to thank many of the people behind the scenes who helped make acquisitions and investments possible. You know who you are, and you all have my deepest thanks," he said as he tipped his glass to the room.

The day was over and Amos was about to go to the hotel. Cullen motioned to him. A wrapped package sat on the table. "Amos, if you would see that Mister MacTavish receives this," he said. "It is from a great many people."

Amos, Riley and Jacob spent a couple of more days in town, but as New Year's came around they went to Rock River to celebrate the incoming year with the MacTavishs. As he usually did, a few minutes before midnight Mac went to his cabinet to get a bottle of the "good stuff", fine Scottish whiskey. Amos, however, stopped him. "Sit down laddie," Amos said with a chuckle and motioned toward a chair. "This time the 'good stuff' is on us." From a box hidden beneath the coat he had left piled by the front door, Amos pulled out the wrapped package and handed it to Mac.

"Amos, lad!" The big man's eyes grew wide as he unwrapped the box. "This is the finest Scotch to be had in all of Scotland! I do nay see how ye can afford to be giving me a bottle of such nectar!" Mac held the bottle as if it were a great treasure.

"It wasn't just me, Mac," Amos said with a smile. "You have a lot of friends that you've shared a great many things with. This is only a small token of their esteem for you." Amos opened the bottle and poured a drink for Mac, his Missus and the rest of his extended family.

There were tears on the blacksmith's cheeks as he held his glass aloft. "Here then is a toast to the year past, friends and family that are nay now here, and to the new year, new friends, new family and love for each and every one," he said and took a sip from his glass. "Oh my lads!" His eyes were as wide as his grin. "I do nay believe I have ever tasted anything so fine."

They laughed and talked well into the small hours of the morning. Laughter often rang and Missus MacTavish would hush them for fear of waking the children. When at last they were ready to go to the barn loft, Missus stood up and held her glass high. "This last drop," she said smiling beautifully, "tis for the three sons I did nay know I had." She emptied her glass, turned and left the room.

The next morning, after "a wee bit" of breakfast, Mac took them to catch the train. He hugged the breath from each one and shook their hands hard enough to rattle their teeth. "Thank ye lads," he said grinning from ear to ear. "Ye be careful! I expect to have a wee sip with ye when the next year rolls in, and each year thereafter for many more to come. And don't ye forget to be stoppin' here when you're passing by."

"Yes Mac, we know," Amos said smiling. "Or Missus will have your hide and probably ours too." They laughed.

The three boarded the train and waved goodbye to Mac, who was still standing on the platform. By early afternoon they were at the ranch house in Carbon. After spending the last couple of weeks in town and on a noisy train, the ranch house was wonderfully quiet. Amos went to make sure his horse hadn't forgotten him and decided to go for a short ride. There was a slight wind from the west as usual, and it followed Amos the short distance he rode. On the way back he quickly remembered the spot on his cheek where he had gotten frostbite. He pulled up a bandanna, doubled it and tied it over the bridge of his nose. When he got back to the ranch house a cup of hot coffee was more than welcome.

27

Some of the hands weren't back yet and some of them that were back were in no shape to eat. Old Charlie the cook set out a pot of coffee, a warm pot of stew along with bread, and a pan of fruit upside-down cake. It was serve yourself and be sure to wash your dishes. Amos, Jacob and Riley sat eating cake. Each one seemed lost in thought.

"What do you think about going off with the Marshall?" Riley finally asked.

"I guess I see it two ways," Amos said as he was knocking thoughts around. "If we go, we have a chance to stop a considerable amount of horse thievery. On the other hand, if something goes wrong here we won't be around to stop it."

"I know what you're saying," Riley said and shrugged. "But we won't be so far away that we can't get back within a day or so. I guess I favor going with the stipulation that we aren't gone too long and we can leave if we need to. That way we get can back in time to check out the count at the roundup."

"Gentlemen," Jacob, who had been quiet until now, said. "I should have little to say about this, but I believe Riley has a good plan. I want you to be exceptionally careful as these men are probably more desperate and of a more evil and devious nature than those we have been dealing with. I shall worry a great deal for your safety."

"So that's the plan then?" Amos asked. They both nodded. "I'll have Clancy send word to the Marshall then," Amos said. They sat quietly, staring at their coffee cups for a few minutes. "What do you suppose it is that Cullen wants us to look into over by Laramie Peak?" Amos asked.

"Darned if I know," Riley said and shrugged. "But I'm sure curious enough to take a ride over there as soon as it warms up and find out."

CHAPTER 5

GOOD COFFEE (1878)

January, February and part of March rolled by and there had been little to do but the usual repairs and checking on cows. A few calves had been born, but nothing compared to the numbers that would come in April. A message came from Cullen requesting that Amos, Jacob and Riley go to the Laramie Peak Ranch, or LP as it was known. The ranch was near Laramie Peak, for which it was named. The peak itself and numerous other places including the fort, the town, and the river were named for a French fur trapper who had died near the peak around 1820. His name was thought to have been Jacque LaRamie, although no one really knew if the first name was correct. The reporters had needed a name that sounded French and Jacque was it. His death was something of a mystery since he was only about thirty years of age and in good shape. Many thought the Arapaho Indians had killed him for his possessions, but the Indians strongly denied this. In almost sixty years since the event nothing concrete had been proven.

Because most of the TIC horses had not had new shoes since fall, it was decided to ride to Medicine Bow where they could pick up supplies and then ride on to Rock River and have Mac shoe all the horses. They stopped to talk to Ted Brow.

"The man you're going to see is Ned Hogan," Brow said as he handed them a map. "He and Cullen worked together, and when Cullen decided to start a ranch Hogan thought it would be a good idea and did the same thing up by Laramie Peak. He's a tough, wiry little guy who could swing the spike hammer all day when they were laying track. They're good friends, and Cullen has helped him through some hard times. Cullen says he's very cautious and very goodhearted. I think you should take good care of him."

Along with the map Brow handed them a copy of a bank draft for more than enough money to cover shoeing six horses. "I know the big guy thinks he owes you something," he said. "But he doesn't owe the ranch anything and we pay our bills. The money is already in his account at Cullen's Bank." Brow winked and said, "Just be sure to hide this copy where he won't find it until you get gone."

"Better yet," Jacob smiled and said, "I shall give it to his wife upon our departure." The rest of them chuckled.

The next morning they drew supplies for a couple of weeks, and took plenty of time to fit the pack saddles and balance the packs. It was about forty five miles from Rock River to the LP Ranch and they planned to stop for one night along the way. Their experiences in the Red Desert had left them a bit gun shy when it came to weather and each of them had a pack horse with more than adequate provisions, plus one additional pack horse to be left with Mac. They left before noon to go to Rock River, got a deer along the way and lashed it to the extra pack horse. Even with the deer as an offering, when they entered the yard they were met with a barrage of snowballs from the children. Mac swung the door of the barn open and motioned them in.

"Quickly lads!" he cried out and laughed heartily as they rode in. "Tis nay safe for ye to be confronting an army such as that. They have had me surrounded and pinned down here since noon." He laughed as he untied the deer and easily lifted it to be hung from one of the rafters. "Even with such capable reinforce-ments as yourselves, I am afraid we are outnumbered by three wee children and a wee baby."

Riley brushed the snow from his coat. "Well, at least they won't starve us out," he said and pointed toward the deer. "We can always cook it over your forge."

"Aye, there is that," Mac said as he grinned broadly. "Or, even-tually my Missus, whom I now believe is directing their attack, will have to call them in for supper." When the horses were unsaddled and wiped down, the big blacksmith set about shoeing them. The other three put their bed rolls in the loft. Amos did what he could to help, and Mac had just finished the last horse when, as predicted, the children were called in. After it was safe, they walked to the house just as the sun set behind the Medicine Bow Mountains. Mac had just taken off his hat and turned around, only to be hit square in the chest with a large snowball from his Missus. She giggled as he easily lifted her off the floor then hugged her. "Did I not tell ye that she is the General in charge of the attack on my barn and my person?" He laughed and grinned at his three friends. "Laddies," he tried to sound serious as he held his huge hands up, "I'm afraid we shall have to surrender or go without supper!" Amos, Jacob and Riley held their hands up in mock surrender as they marched behind Mac, in step, toward the dining table.

The meal was elegant in its simplicity, and far above adequate in its quantity. Amos could not help but notice that the twin boys each ate as much as he did. They were not yet ten years old, but were growing so quickly that they would soon be bigger than Amos, or either one of his two friends. It would however be a long time before they caught up to their father, who of course ate twice as much as anyone. March nights can be cold in Wyoming, but the heat from the forge kept the barn pleasantly warm. They slept well that night.

In the morning the temperature was well below freezing, but the clear skies and lack of wind promised a day in the forties. The plan was to ride east until they came to the Laramie River; they would then follow it to the northeast where the river turned and went almost due east. There they would find a place to camp. The next day they would ride northeast to the Palmer Canyon wagon road and follow it to the Cottonwood Park wagon road which they would follow until they came to the LP Ranch. The first day of the trip they would cover about twenty five miles and follow relatively flat ground. The second day would involve less distance, but was more uphill. As evening set in they found a good place to camp on the lee side of a hill along the river. There was open water, and grass for the horses was abundant, although there was not much nutritional value in it at that time of year.

There was plenty of dry driftwood for a fire so they could have hot coffee. The evening meal consisted of the deer roast Missus MacTavish had given them, warmed over the fire, and the slice of apple pie she had made sure each of them had. Amos lay on his bed roll looking at the stars.

"Spring comes," Jacob said. "The hawk begins to fly."

"What do you mean by that?" Riley asked.

"If you look in the northern sky you'll see several stars that form a W; that would be Cassiopeia," Jacob said pointing skyward. "Just behind that is a constellation that the white world calls Bootes. The Children of the Mountain call it The Hawk. Each year in the spring it begins to move across the sky. They say that when the hawk begins to fly, spring will soon follow."

"Well, it looks a lot more like a hawk than a boot to me," Riley said as he yawned. "I hope they're right, I've had enough winter for one year." In five minutes he was asleep.

The next morning they rose and heated up some coffee along with biscuits and beans before they got going. They rode northeast away from the Laramie River. In a couple of miles they had crossed Duck Creek and a few miles later had come to the Cottonwood Park Road. There was snow on the ground but a wagon had followed the road and the tracks were melted out so that traveling was easy. By midafternoon they had come to the LP Ranch.

They rode up to the ranch house making enough noise so that anyone could have heard them coming. Amos stayed on his horse as he hollered to see if anyone was there. A rather small man with a rather large double barreled shotgun came out. His face was as hard as the granite that surrounded his ranch.

"If you boys are looking for work," he said. "I'm not hiring anyone." His eyes stayed on them, and his thumb stayed on the hammers of the shotgun.

"Well dang it, Mister Hogan!" Riley said as he flashed his best grin. "Mister Cullen sent us all the way up here for nothing. Guess we better head home boys." He started to turn his horse.

"I guess you'd be Riley," Hogan said as his thumb moved away from the hammers. "And you would be Amos Moss, and you would be Jacob Hanley." Each man nodded as he spoke their names. A smile crossed his face as he said, "Well don't just sit there. You can put your horses in the barn over there. There's plenty of room in the bunkhouse and supper will be coming up in about an hour. Oh yeah, my name is Ned. The only one that calls me Mister Hogan is the banker, and it usually means he wants more of my money."

They stowed their gear, laid out their bed rolls and got cleaned up. There were only two ranch hands, Burke and Barry Hogan, the sons of Ned Hogan, and they proved to be quite friendly. The hour went by and Amos, Jacob and Riley followed the Hogan brothers to the ranch house. It was not large and had only eight seats around the dining table. Ned introduced his wife. Her name was Hilda, but everyone called her Mother Hogan. She wore her braided brown hair in a bun on top of her head. She had happy blue eyes, and was about as wide as she was tall. She was very cheerful as she set a sliced roast with vegetables on the table. There was fresh baked bread with wild berry jam and the best coffee Amos had drunk since he'd left GrandMoss in Arkansas. Amos had always loved good coffee and this was the kind that should not ever, under any circumstances, be wasted. He was trying to figure out how to get another cup when Mother Hogan came in with apple strudel for each of them and poured more coffee without Amos having to say a word. She even left the pot on the table. Amos was sure he had come to the right place.

When supper was over and the dishes were cleared, Ned Hogan pulled out a bag of tobacco and filled his pipe. He lit it, leaned back in his chair and looked at the three of them. The tobacco smell reminded Amos of Tom Sherman Senior back at the livery stable in Laramie.

"I guess I better tell you about what's going on. You're probably going to think I'm crazy," he said as he shrugged his shoulders slightly. "About once a month a cow disappears up on Laramie Peak. In the summer there's not much for tracks, so I would figure it was Indians or rustlers. Problem is that it doesn't seem like they would take just one cow, and they always leave the gut pile; rustlers wouldn't do that. Now here comes the strange part! In the winter there are tracks everywhere, but they never lead into or away from the area where the cow is killed. They just go all

33

over around the cow and that's it; except that the tracks are round and about a foot across! You can think I'm crazy for tonight, but tomorrow I'll take you up to show you. Another cow disappeared three days ago."

Amos had been slow to eat his strudel, making sure he had adequate excuse for another cup of coffee. Jacob knew what was going on and raised an eyebrow as he looked at Amos. "I guess we better get to bed then, Ned," he said as he smirked at Amos. "Come on Amos, any more coffee and you'll be awake all night. Not to mention the cold air you'll be letting in the bunkhouse when you run in and out." Amos scowled at him, but they went to the bunkhouse anyway.

"Well, I'm completely confused," Riley said as he pulled his boots off. "But with food that good, I'm going to be willing to work on this problem for a long time." He chuckled as he got into bed.

"Good food, good people, good coffee, and an interesting problem to work on," Jacob said smiling. "This has the potential to end up being fun."

CHAPTER 6

WATCHED (1878)

The sky was just getting gray, which meant it was about six in the morning, when the Hogan brothers rolled out of bed and started pulling their boots on. "Better get a move on boys," Burke said. "Mom will have breakfast going by now, and when she rings the bell, she expects you to be sitting at the table within about a minute."

Barry chuckled and said, "Make sure your hands are clean or she'll send you back out to wash up. By the time you do that your breakfast might already be gone."

Everyone washed up and, just as predicted, Mother Hogan rang the bell a few minutes later. They went in to find a huge stack of pancakes along with ham and eggs, and of course the coffee that was even better than Amos remembered. Mother Hogan served everyone, and much to Amos's delight, coffee cups never got below half-full. No one was allowed to leave the table until everything was gone. She did not pack lunches for anyone, but with as much as there had been for breakfast, it was unnecessary.

She would not allow anyone to help with the kitchen work. "I do not want to work on those nasty old cows," she said emphatically, "and I don't need you dusty old men dirtying up my nice clean kitchen. Now you get on out of here before I take the broom to you!" She laughed and her face danced as she spoke. Amos could well imagine that her kitchen was probably the cleanest one he had been around in many years.

The brothers would not be going on the trip, but would be checking cattle along the North Laramie River. The temperature was just below freezing; given the time of year, it was a nice day. Nonetheless, each man tied an extra coat along with their slicker to their saddle. The ranch was at about the same elevation as the Upper River Ranch house and they would be going up another thousand feet in elevation. Laramie Peak is over ten thousand feet high and is easily the highest peak in the area. Because of this, it tends to "catch the clouds" and has its own weather patterns, especially in the spring. That often means snow and heavy cloud cover even when the surrounding area stays clear.

Amos noticed that everyone was carrying repeating rifles so he opted to take his Sharps, which he carried across the saddle. They rode for just over two hours and finally came to a small meadow that sat in a U-shaped cove in the granite rocks. The upper end abutted a granite cliff about sixty feet high and on either side the granite tapered away to ground level. The entire meadow covered less than an acre and was well protected from the wind. It was a place that cattle would naturally be drawn to, but on this day there were none in the area. Ned had them dismount at the low end of the meadow.

"We better walk from here boys," he said as he tied his horse to a scrub pine. "I think you'll want to see this without any horse tracks to mess it up." He walked up the low granite rock that bordered the right side of the meadow. A few feet up he stopped and pointed to a dark patch. "Right there is where the gut pile was. The ravens have pretty well cleaned it up now," he said as he handed a pair of binoculars to Amos. "If you look around you'll see those round tracks I was telling you about. They look bigger now than they really were because the sun has melted them out some. When they were fresh, they were about a foot across."

Amos was used to looking through his spyglass and it took him a few minutes to get the binoculars adjusted. Jacob had brought his own pair which he was sharing with Riley. They looked for several minutes, then went up the rock further and looked some more.

"I've looked at those tracks a hundred times," Ned said. "I'll be damned if I can figure it out! There are no tracks in or out and there's no cave or even a crack in the rocks anyone could get through. I've gone all around the area and I haven't seen another track outside of what you can see from right here."

"Sir, is this the only place that this sort of event has happened?" Jacob asked.

"No," Ned said with a shrug. "There's half a dozen other places about like it around the mountain where the same thing has happened. Each time it's the same."

"I want to get a good close look at those tracks," Riley said. "Is it okay if I go down there and walk around a little bit?"

"Sure, just don't wear your round boots," Amos said as he smiled at Riley. Riley scowled, rolled his eyes and slid down the rock to the meadow.

"Well, if you boys can find your way back," Ned said as he started toward his horse, "I'll head on back. I've got cows to check between here and the house. Don't be late for supper," he said and chuckled. "Mother likes to serve things hot." He straddled his horse and headed away.

Riley continued to walk around, while Jacob circled the rocks around the head of the meadow. Amos went to the opposite side and walked up to a vantage point where he could look down on the tracks. He switched sides several times as the light changed and each time the tracks look different, but no pattern emerged. The three of them spent most of the day walking around trying to find anything that might help them figure out what was happening. By midafternoon the wind had picked up and a few clouds were forming at the top of Laramie Peak. They decided it was a good time to ride back to the ranch house and compare notes.

Little was said on the way back as each of them was deep in thought. They arrived back at the ranch house just as the two Hogan brothers rode up. Ned's horse had already been put away and he was busily pitching hay into the rest of the stalls. "Did you get it all worked out?" he asked as he put the pitchfork away.

"No," Riley replied. "I think we have more questions now than before we got here. But at least we have some better information to make wild guesses with."

"Don't feel too bad," Ned said as he started towards the house. "I've been looking at those tracks since right after I started running cows up here, and I still don't know what's going on."

"Could you tell me how long that has been, Sir?" Jacob asked.

"Ooh," Ned said scratching his chin. "Since about '66 I guess. Best I can tell I've lost about eight or ten cows on the average each year. Last few years its run as high as a dozen, but usually about ten".

"That's a good thirty five hundred bucks!" Riley said as he arched his eyebrows. "I can see why you want to get to the bottom of it."

"Yeah," Ned said as he shrugged. "Did you come to any conclusions today?"

"Not yet," Amos said. "We're going to talk about it after supper tonight. You said there were several other places where this same thing has happened. Could you show us those places?"

"Sure," Ned replied. "I can't go tomorrow, but I can have one of the boys take you."

"That's good enough…" The last part was drowned out by Mother Hogan ringing the dinner bell. Supper was pretty much the same as the night before and just as good. Amos managed to come up with three cups of coffee before Jacob shooed him out again. They sat talking in the bunkhouse and getting whatever additional information they could from the Hogan brothers.

"I couldn't figure out any pattern to the tracks," Amos said. "Except that they tend to radiate out from where the cow was. There are several sets that seem to end at the bottom of the cliff, and others that go over to both sides. They all stop right there and there is no return track. I couldn't find any sign of another track after that."

"I think there are two different sets of tracks," Riley said. "Most of the tracks are made by a lighter person, but some of them sink in the snow deeper so it must be a bigger guy. That and the tracks aren't just the round holes; there is a second track on top of each one that looks to be round too, but they're another six inches on all sides. It looks like a pant cuff mark or a boot top, but it seems like it sticks further out than it should."

"I walked around all the rocks at the top of the cliff," Jacob said. "There are some scrape marks like someone walked up there, but nothing that resembles the round tracks in the bottom."

Amos looked at the Hogan brothers. "Did you guys walk around up there at all lately?" he asked.

"Yeah," Barry said with a shrug. "When we first found the site I walked around the whole thing and I didn't find anything. That was before Pop told us to stay away from there. Those could be my tracks. I'm sorry if I messed you guys up."

"You could not have known," Jacob said. "In any case, the marks did not appear to be those that would usually be made by boots such as you wear."

The next day Burke Hogan guided them around the area. There were six additional sites that were similar to the one they had visited. Some faced north or west and would have been used by cattle in summer. One site faced east and would catch the morning sun. Still another faced southeast and had been used by cattle recently. Each site had a number of cow bones around. There were skulls, neck, and lower leg bones, but no upper body and limb bones. All sites had flint chips and showed past occupancy by Indians, but it appeared they had not used it for many years. The day quickly passed, and by midafternoon they were at least twelve miles from the ranch house. The trail was good; even so, they had to move right along to get back in time for supper. They had just ridden in when Mother Hogan rang the dinner bell. The food was hot and she wasn't waiting for anyone. Saddles were hastily removed, horses fed and face washing done before the four of them ran for the house.

The food was superb, as usual, although there was little conversation through the meal. Ned Hogan must've noticed it. After supper and the traditional lighting of his pipe, he tipped back his chair and looked at the four men. "So tell me what you figured out, boys," he said as he looked through his little cloud of pipe smoke. "I can see that you're pretty deep in thought."

"There are several obvious things that I'm sure you have noticed, Sir," Jacob began. "The cattle use the different areas according to the time of year." Ned nodded. "The bones left behind show that the head, lower legs and tail were removed and discarded. The skulls have been broken so the brain could be removed, probably to be used for leather tanning. Certainly no predator would have done that, and it is unlikely that a rustler would, although Indians may have. Further, there are few signs that stone implements were used, so it is unlikely that this is the work of Indians. Finally, the numbers of bones show that cattle are taken more frequently during the winter months. There are fewer bones in the areas where cattle would be in the summer than there are in areas where they would be in the winter. Possibly, whoever is taking your cattle finds more wildlife to eat in summer."

Riley raised his hand slightly and said, "The trails around the area don't show any tracks that we can't account for. The side trails don't seem to go anywhere out of what would be ordinary for cows. I don't think we are dealing with more than a few people. There would be more sign if we were."

Ned blew out a cloud of smoke. "So what do you think Amos?" he asked.

"The tracks still have me puzzled," Amos said. "There is something there that I just haven't quite put together yet. There is one thing I do know." His voice dropped to a whisper. "We were being watched today."

CHAPTER 7

COLD ASHES (1878)

A fter supper they returned to the bunkhouse. "Well, I guess you gave him something to think about," Riley said. "I don't know if we were watched, but something seemed different. I just figured it was my imagination getting the best of me."

"I would never doubt that your imagination could get the best of you," Jacob said matter-of-factly. "However, I do know that we were watched. I saw movement several times that could not be explained by wildlife."

"Are you boys serious?" Barry asked. "Do you think maybe we should get a bunch of guys together and go up there and see what we can roust out?"

"I think that's probably the one thing that we should not do," Amos sighed and said. "If whoever, or whatever, has gotten along all these years without being caught, then they probably have things figured out enough to avoid a crowd of people that don't know where they're going. What we're going to have to do is get sneaky and see if we can catch them off guard."

"It's a good thing we have our favorite sneaky Indian with us then," Riley said grinning at Jacob, who scowled back. "From what I understand he can sneak up on just about anybody; well, at least Amos." Amos joined Jacob in scowling at Riley, who just laughed and went to bed.

They rose early the next day, ate quickly, and were on their way to Laramie Peak just as the sun rose. Overnight there had been a light dusting of snow and they hoped to find the tracks of anyone in the area. In a full day of riding and climbing around on the mountain they found no tracks except a few deer, elk and coyotes. They arrived back at the ranch after dark, cold, tired and frustrated. Mother Hogan had been kind enough to set aside three plates of food and a pot of coffee for them. Despite Jacob's harassment, Amos was enjoying a third cup of coffee. Ned Hogan joined them just as they finished eating.

"Well, what did you boys find today?" he asked. "By your faces and the lack of conversation, I suspect it wasn't much."

"The fact that we found no one is somewhat disheartening," Jacob said. "That fact, however, tells us that whomever or whatever is up there, is operating nocturnally."

Amos had been staring into his coffee cup, now his head came full upright. "Ned, have you or your boys ever seen any kind of light or smoke up there, like a campfire or a torch?" he asked.

Ned thought for a minute then said, "No, nothing I was ever sure about. Of course, the boys have spent a lot more time up there than I have. Maybe you should go ask them."

"We could," Riley said, "if we could get Amos away that coffee pot!"

"Yeah, I've noticed that he does like Mother's coffee," Ned said with a smile. "I can't say that I blame him. Take some with you. You can bring the cup back in in the morning."

That was agreeable to Amos and the three of them went to the bunkhouse. The Hogan brothers were relaxing on their bunks. Burke was reading a month old newspaper, and Barry had a dime novel. Amos explained his question to them.

"Well," Barry said as he laid down his novel, "a few years ago in April we got hung out up there helping a heifer have a calf. Up on the mountain I thought I saw some light, but I figured it was just the way the moon was shining on the snow. I can point out just where it was; you can see it from here." He returned to reading his novel. Amos could not help noticing the title, "Bill Hickok, Wild Gunman of the West". He wondered if there was more than one sentence of truth in the whole book.

Apparently the light dusting of snow the previous day had just been a warning. That night a spring blizzard rolled in and left six inches of wet heavy snow at the ranch house and it was deeper further up on Laramie Peak. It was overcast and still snowing lightly after breakfast. There would be little to do on Laramie Peak that day, so the three men volunteered to help with the cattle. In its own way just being a cowboy again felt good to Amos. Most of the day had been spent riding from one group of cattle to another and sometimes helping with a newborn calf. There had been plenty of time to think as he rode along. Late in the day, just as the sun was setting, the clouds lifted enough that Barry was able to point out where he had seen the possible lights.

That evening, after supper, Amos sat enjoying another cup of the coffee that should never be wasted. "I'm thinking," he said to Riley and Jacob, "that we need to be up where we can see the mountain on a good, clear, calm night. This snow will go off in a few days, and we could sneak up there pretty late and see if we can pick out smoke coming from somewhere."

"I was thinking the same thing," Riley said. "But I'm willing to wait for it to warm up a little."

"I would concur, especially with the latter part of that statement," Jacob said and smiled at Riley. "I believe we should view the west, south, and east sides of the peak, since it is unlikely that anyone would camp on the north side at this time of year." The plan was set.

For the next several days they helped with the cattle while a warm spring wind cleared away most of the snow. After several days the wind became still late in the afternoon and they decided it would be the right time to try the plan. In twilight they rode close to the base of the peak. Each one chose a vantage point that would let them see almost a third of the mountain. Riley went to the west side and Jacob to the east, while Amos took the south side of the peak.

It was well after dark, his horse was out of sight, and Amos was sitting behind a scrub pine in a cleft between two large granite boulders. Despite the shelter of the trees and his large buffalo coat, the cold was beginning to creep in. He had begun to think his plan was faulty. At two o'clock in the morning he decided to make one last scan through his spyglass and then call it a night. He looked toward the peak and saw fine wisps of smoke. He was not sure if his eyes had deceived him and he was just seeing a bit of cloud. He watched for nearly an hour and was sure the smoke was coming from behind some rocks. He heard a noise behind him and turned to see Riley coming up. "You're not near as sneaky as Jacob," he said as Riley joined him.

"No he is not," Jacob said as he stepped from behind the same rocks Riley had just passed. "I assume you two have noticed the same plume of smoke that I have. From the east there is a small amount of light to be seen against the rocks." They both looked at Jacob and shook their heads.

"Yeah," Riley said. "You sneaky…anyway. But what are we going to do about it?"

"Nothing tonight," Amos said looking through his spyglass. "We've got the information we needed and we aren't set up to go climbing up that mountain tonight. I think we should get the right gear and figure on doing this on another night. We can go tomorrow night, if the weather stays good."

Riley checked his watch. "Gee whiz, its three o'clock in the morning," he said in mock surprise. "You guys are a bad influence on me." He flashed a grin. "Well, at least we know what time they start their fire."

"And where," Jacob said thinking out loud. "If we are very careful we should be in the area at approximately this time tomorrow night."

"We're going to need to be very careful," Amos said still looking into his spyglass. "They already know we're here from watching us the other day. I hate to split up, but I think we're going to have to. If they see us coming they'll just move off. By splitting up we have a chance of getting a look at them, even if we can't get the jump on them."

Everyone agreed; they watched for almost an hour and then headed back to the ranch house and some warmth. They had ridden by moonlight, but sunup was only a couple of hours away by the time they got back and took care of their horses. Amos would usually have gone to bed, but the thought of Mother Hogan's wonderful breakfast kept him awake. He could always sleep, but he did not want to waste the chance at good food and especially coffee that was that good. They ate breakfast and reported their findings to Ned Hogan. He said he had seen the smoke before, but had always thought it was just wisps of fog. The two brothers drew maps of the easiest ways to get up the mountain and they corresponded very closely to what Amos, Jacob and Riley had already come up with. There was, however, a shortcut on the east side that Jacob had not been able to see from his vantage point.

After breakfast they got the gear they would need, including some hard hemp rope that could be wrapped around their leather boots to give them better traction than their leather soles. In midafternoon they decided to sleep in preparation for the night's activities. It was well after dark when Amos awoke. Mother Hogan had not rung the dinner bell and the Hogan brothers had not come in the bunkhouse to disturb them. It was nearly nine in the evening when they went in the house hoping to find a little bit of something to eat before they left. Much to their delight, Mother Hogan had three large plates, heaping full, in the warming oven of her huge wood stove. Of course there was a pot of coffee, and Amos stocked up.

It would be a two hour ride to where they planned to start up the mountain. Then it would be another three hours to climb the mountain. If all went well they would converge at the same time on the area where they had seen the fire the night before. They wore their heavy buffalo coats for the ride, but left them draped over their horses for their warmth. They each carried their Winchester rifles, since the Sharps rifles were almost twice as heavy and the extra range they provided would probably not be needed. Between their pistols and the Winchester rifles, each man could fire about half of a fifty round box of 44.40 ammunition before having to reload. Each of them carried a spare box of ammunition.

They rode to the edge of the timber and then waited until the moon rose. The climb up the mountain would be approximately the same for each man. However, Riley and Jacob had further to ride, so they agreed to start the climb at eleven. Amos got to his position with time to spare, and watched through his spyglass but could see nothing. This did not surprise him since he had not seen the smoke until about two in the morning. At eleven he began his climb. It was easy enough going part of the way, but then the frost settled and the rocks started getting slick under the leather soles of his boots. He stopped and made several wraps of rope across the forward sole of his boot. It made traction amazingly better.

At four in the morning he was approaching the large rock that the fire had been behind. He could have gone faster, but he was doing everything he could to be quiet. He quietly chambered a round in his rifle and eased around the end of the rocks. There was no fire, but someone was hunched over the fire pit pushing the cold ashes with a stick. It was Jacob.

CHAPTER 8

JACQUE LARAMIE (1878)

"**H**ello Amos," Jacob said but did not turn around as he continued poking around the fire pit. "They were here last night, but they have been gone for at least twelve hours. By the bones, I believe they have been eating beef. With just moonlight it is difficult to read the tracks, but I believe there are at least two of them and one of them is significantly larger than the others. And Riley is just about to get here."

Amos walked over and a few seconds later heard a Winchester rifle cycling in a round. "Hands over your heads!" Riley said loudly. "Turn around slow."

"It was the white eyes!" Jacob exclaimed as he turned around and pointed at Amos. "Arrest him before he gets away Marshall!"

"It was the Indian, General," Amos said pointing at Jacob. "Sound the charge! I think he's on the warpath!"

Riley shook his head and sat down on his haunches, his gun resting over his knees. "Crap" was all he said as he took the shell out of the chamber of his rifle. Amos and Jacob were laughing, pointing at Riley and laughing some more. "After all that sneaking around," Riley said forlornly, "and figuring I had it made, this is what I get." He just shook his head. Jacob and Amos were laughing again.

Eventually the laughter died down. "I recall a day over by Bradley Peak that felt a little like this." Amos said as he wiped tears from his eyes. "At least this time we got a laugh out of it. Well, at least two of us did." He laughed again.

"If you two can get a rein on yourselves," Riley said. He tried to scowl, but started chuckling. "Could you tell me what we're going to do now?"

"I believe we should wait for it to get light so we can examine the tracks and the surrounding area." Jacob said trying to sound serious. "From what I can see this is not a permanent campsite. Logically then, the two or more people who were here last night are moving from campsite to campsite. It is also possible that they may be part of a larger group."

They agreed; it was approaching four in the morning, but daylight was still three hours away. They did not want to walk around the campsite for fear of destroying valuable information. They could do little but stand in the coldness of predawn at high elevation and wish for the sun. Even though it seemed like it would never rise, the sun finally touched the top of the peak. It was easy to see why this was a chosen campsite. The first few rays of light quickly began to melt the frost on the granite cliffs and in a few minutes it had warmed considerably. The tracks in the dirt around the campfire were a confused jumble. They were, however, moccasin tracks. In a split in the rock, where the sun was not yet able to get, there were tracks in the snow. They could see that one print was slightly smaller than average and the other was nearly half again larger than Amos's. They followed the tracks for a short distance until they disappeared on the same granite ledge Amos had followed to come up. They looked around for another two hours but found nothing more of interest, except a hidden cleft in the rocks where a great many bones had been thrown. There were the expected cow bones, as well as those of deer, elk and buffalo. Surprisingly there were also the bones of mountain lions, wolves and bears, including two very large grizzly bear skulls.

It was approaching noon when they decided to head back down. Riley went down the western side, while Jacob went east and Amos started back to the south. Amos walked along the ledge they had inspected earlier and went along until he got to the pile of rocks that marked the point where he could get down. He had stopped for one last look at the scenery when something grabbed him from behind. He thought it was a bear. Huge hairy arms crushed the air from him and he could not move his arms. He kicked his feet with no effect. As he started to blackout he chambered a round in his rifle and pulled the trigger. At the noise whatever it was grabbed him by the shoulders and started to throw him off the ledge. From behind him he heard someone holler, "non-non-non!" and something else that he did not understand, but it sounded like the language of the Children of the Mountain.

He was thrown on the ledge instead of off of it. The rifle was ripped from his hand and dropped to the ground. He heard a shot and a second shot and Riley yelling, "The next one kills you!"

His breath returned and his mind was clearing. He saw that "the bear" was actually a very large man in a buffalo coat and hat that had the horns sticking out of it. He was huge, larger even than Mac, and he appeared to be Indian. "Non-non-non!" Amos heard the voice again and a much smaller man, no larger than Ned Hogan, waved his arms and stepped in front of the giant. "Non-non-non!" he said again. "Non shoot, mon ami, mon ami, non shoot!" He pointed to the giant. "Mon fils, mon fils" The voice reminded Amos of Maurice de Mortimer.

Amos did not know what was going on. Riley quickly came to his side and handed him one of his pistols. "I don't know what the hell's going on," Riley said. His eyes were wide. "But what he said first sure sounded a lot like what the Sheep Eaters say."

"It is that, plus some French and some English," Jacob said as he approached from the east with his rifle leveled at hip height. "I believe he is trying to tell you not to shoot, that he is a friend, and the quite large man is his son."

Amos rose and caught his breath for a few minutes while he tried to make sense of things, then he retrieved his rifle. It appeared undamaged, but he would check it out when he could. He gave Riley his pistol back. "Not even Mac ever squeezed me like that. I'm going to be sore," he said still puffing. "Jacob, do you think you can talk to them?"

"I'm not putting my gun down," Riley exclaimed and sounded angry, "until you can tell me that everything is all right!"

"Agreed," Jacob said. He began speaking to the smaller man. In a few minutes he turned. "I believe you can put your weapons down now," he said as he nodded to Riley. "But I believe I would keep it close at hand, just in case."

Amos and Riley leaned against a boulder while Jacob and the older man talked for nearly an hour. Riley had lowered his weapon but still kept it cradled in his arms, although he had lowered the hammer to half cock, he had not taken the cartridge from the chamber and he had replaced the two cartridges he had fired.

Finally Jacob came over to them. "This is a most amazing turn of events!" His voice held wonderment. "The older man's name is Jacque LaRamie!" Jacob pronounced the last name "La Ray Me".

"He can't be Jacque Laramie." Riley sounded irritated. "Jacque Laramie has been dead for about sixty years now. Besides that, if he was Jacque Laramie, he would be about a hundred years old. That guy's old, but he's not that old."

"He is not the same Jacque Laramie that you are thinking of." Jacob was trying very hard to explain everything. "He is the son of Marcel LaRamie. No one actually ever knew the real first name of the Jacque LaRamie for whom the peak is named. The reporters needed a first name and Jacque sounded French. His son says it was really Marcel. He says his father disappeared on this mountain because he wanted to, not because he was attacked by the Arapahoe. There were still some Shoshone Indians on this mountain at that time. They were known as the Buffalo Eaters because of their diet, just as my people were known as the Sheep Eaters because of their diet." Jacob was talking very quickly and trying very hard to keep the story straight. "Old Marcel took a Shoshone wife and the older man is their progeny. In time, Jacque grew up and also took a Shoshone wife and the big man is their son. Marcel and Jacque both lost their wives and several of their children when almost all of the tribe died from smallpox. They apparently had some immunity to it, as many white people do, and this was passed from father to son. Marcel lived well into old age, although Jacque is not sure how old he was. The few remaining tribal members joined a group of Shoshone that were passing by and left. Old Marcel named his son Jacque because he heard the story of his own death and figured there should be a real Jacque LaRamie. The big man's name is also Marcel LaRamie, after his grandfather, but he calls himself, Standing Bull," Jacob said with a smile. "Obviously the name fits him."

"You're telling me that family has been up here for a hundred years?" Amos was incredulous.

"Since about 1820, actually," Jacob said. "They are not even sure what year this is."

"How did they stay out of sight for sixty years?" Riley asked.

"That is very interesting," Jacob said. "Obviously they know the area extremely well. They have a number of caves, overhangs and other campsites that they move back and forth through. They don't stay at any one place long enough to make it look well used. That's why we missed them; they did see us, but they were about to move on anyway. They have fires only late at night and prepare enough food for the next day. They never stay at any one place more than a couple of days."

"Well, that explains them," Riley said with a shrug. "But what about the problem of killing cattle?"

"They, uh…look at it a little differently than we do," Jacob said, carefully putting his words together. "They were here well before the ranch, the cattle, and for that matter most of the white people. The cattle are encroaching on the land that once fed the elk, deer, buffalo and all the other animals that they used and relied on. They have not minded sharing the land with the white people, but they feel like they should be paid for their loss in some form or another. Since the white people have taken away the wildlife, it seems only fair to them to occasionally take a cow to eat, in lieu of their normal animals."

"I think you're going to have a difficult time convincing Ned Hogan of that," Riley said.

"There might be a way," Amos said, thinking out loud. "I don't know about you two, but I haven't seen any predator tracks to speak of since we've been here. A few coyotes, but no mountain lions, bears or wolves. It's late enough in the year that the bears should be out. I suspect that these two are the reason for that. Now, I don't know how many cattle Ned could expect to lose to predators, but I'll bet it's a lot more than he actually does. He runs less than half as many cattle as the TIC and he loses only a couple to predators each year. The TIC has a lot of cowboys out there to shoot at the predators and it loses thirty or forty. A ranch the size of the TIC, with the normal number of cowhands, would probably lose fifty or more. Ned said he is losing about ten cows a year to these guys, so it looks to me like he is further ahead to have these guys up here hunting predators than he would be if they were gone." Amos looked at the other two. "It looks like, if they could get friendly, Ned could provide them with decent guns, a few supplies and the occasional cow, and he would come out way ahead."

"It might just work!" Jacob said excitedly. "Let me see what we can work out."

"Before you do," Amos said as he held up a hand to stop him, "be sure they understand that all of this will have to be cleared with Ned Hogan."

"Of course, Amos," Jacob said and went off to talk with the two mountain men. They sat cross legged on the ground speaking several different languages and making many hand signs. The afternoon wore on, and it was getting close to three o'clock when Amos reminded Jacob that they still had to get back to the ranch.

"Yes, yes, we are just getting done," Jacob said as he waved a hand at Amos. In a few moments Jacob rose; he extended his arms and much to Amos's surprise they did nearly the same departing gestures that the Sheep Eaters always did. "Fascinating, very fascinating." Jacob's voice still carried excitement. "They are quite willing to work with Mister Hogan. In fact they have wanted to do so for some time, but were afraid to approach him. On several occasions they have been within a few yards of the ranch buildings, but became afraid and returned to the mountain. There is so much to tell Amos, and so much more to discover. I don't know where to begin."

"Well, begin with this," Amos said as he pointed to the valley below. "We better be getting down off this mountain. Maybe we can get Ned to come up here and talk with them."

"Oh, much better than that," Jacob said grinning from ear to ear. "They have agreed to come down and talk with Ned and his family. We are to take the offer to Ned, and if he agrees or even if he doesn't, in two days they will meet me further down the hill where the round tracks are."

"Yeah, what about those tracks?" Riley asked.

"That's easily enough explained," Jacob said. "They made those by wearing something like round snowshoes with a short round piece of wood attached to the bottom. They could walk forward or backward and the tracks would appear the same. When they killed a cow, Standing Bull would carry the quarters to the edge of the meadow, where they could be thrown to the rocks and carried away without leaving tracks. They would always wrap the quarters in an old hide so there would be no blood showing. Occasionally they would take the quarters up a cliff face on a rope. They were making tracks everywhere to confuse anyone who came on the scene. They worked at night and when the wind was blowing, so the tracks would be obscured and difficult to read. They are quite ingenious."

The deal was taken back to Ned Hogan and, much to Jacob's relief, it was accepted. The two men met and Jacob translated. It was good to see that they hit it off quite well. Jacque LaRamie spoke very little, and very broken, English. It was however easy to see that he would pick more of it up quickly. Only Standing Bull remained aloof.

Once everything was settled it was time to head back to Medicine Bow. Amos truly hated to leave behind the best coffee he'd had in so many years. Mother Hogan tried to explain how to make it, but it was as lost on him as Jim Hickok's cross draw had been a decade earlier.

CHAPTER 9

HAGGIS (1878)

It had taken less than a month to figure out the problem that had been plaguing Ned Hogan for most of a decade, and a peaceful and beneficial solution had been reached. Amos talked about the work they were doing with Jacob and Riley as they rode along. The discussion became drawn out, sometimes practical, sometimes philosophical and sometimes comical. Each time they all came to the same conclusion. It was not so much that other people could not do the same things, but that they did not want to take the time to do it. And most people were afraid of the firearms aspect of what they were doing. In reality, excluding the Indian battles, in eight years the three of them had fired only a handful of shots at people, and only a half dozen or so of them were dead. All had been given the opportunity to surrender peaceably but had refused it, and most of it had been self-defense. All of the dead men had been thieves, if not murderers and the general public was far better off without them. In the end it seemed that they were doing much the same thing as Sheriff Nathan Tower, simply on a different scale and in a much larger area.

That night they camped again along the Laramie River in the same place that they had camped on their way to the LP Ranch. It was now April and the lower snow was melting. The river had risen slightly and had become murky. Even if there had been high water it would have presented no problem, since there was no place that they actually had to cross it.

The plan had been to ride directly to Medicine Bow and check in with Ted Brow. The more they thought about it, a quick stop to see Mac MacTavish and his family seemed like the right thing to do. Even though it wasn't all that far to Rock River they rose early and got going. They wanted to get there well before evening. By midafternoon they were riding up the road to the blacksmith's shop. They had been laughing and joking as they went along; suddenly the sound of a loud scream split the air. They spurred their horses, galloped into the front yard with guns drawn, jumped to a dismount to hear the sound coming from inside the house. Amos burst through the front door with both of his Schofields in hand, followed by Riley with his guns drawn. Amos made one step in the door and stopped frozen in his tracks only to be knocked nearly off his feet by Riley, who stopped and stood slack-jawed. Jacob stepped calmly through the door and grinned broadly.

In front of them was a six-foot ten inch, three hundred pound Scotsman wearing a tall bear skin hat and dressed fully in red plaid. Part of it looked like a skirt to Amos, who was standing and staring with his mouth agape. The sound was coming from tubes that came from a bag held under Mac's left arm. He was blowing into another tube while playing something that looked like a flute that came from the bottom of the bag. Missus MacTavish, who of course had been surprised quickly held a finger to her lips to quiet them, then rose and hugged each of them. The children hugged each of their uncles, but did not say a word. Mac flashed a smile, but the sound did not stop. Instead it went on for another thirty minutes. Amos had begun to feel the rhythm and vibration of the music and found it to be stirring. Finally, Mac's face had become quite red and he stopped playing.

"This is delightful," Jacob said and clapped his hands. "I have not heard the pipes since I studied in Edinburgh. That would be the Tartan of the MacTavish clan, would it not?"

"Aye, it would be," Mac said as he grinned broadly. "And a proud one it is too!"

"A Highland MacTavish Tartan I would guess, by the way the blue mixes with the reds," Jacob said looking closely at the bagpipes. "The final piece would be the song of your clan if I'm not mistaken." Mac nodded. "What is the occasion?" Jacob asked.

"Why, boys, ye must have lost track of time," Missus said and smiled beautifully. "Tis Easter and my MacTavish always plays his pipes on Easter, Robert Burn's birthday and the Fourth of July. And he plays for nay less than an hour each time. Aye, it does take me back to my childhood each time." She looked wistful.

Riley had finally gotten his jaw working again. "But why do you wear a skirt when you're playing that thing?" he asked. His eyes were still wide.

"I can forgive ye for being Irish, but aire ye daft too?" Mac feigned anger. "Tis not a skirt, tis a kilt. Tis the dress uniform of all the Scottish Clans."

"Gentlemen," Jacob said trying not to laugh, "I'm not sure you realize that you are still holding your guns, but if you two will put them away, I will be happy to go back outside and explain this to you." Amos's face was red as he put his pistols back in their holsters. As he followed Jacob and Riley outside, they could hear Missus MacTavish start giggling. She was soon joined by her children and then by the roaring laughter of her husband. Jacob briefly explained that each clan had its colors, and that they were woven into a plaid, called a tartan and worn by each member of the clan. "I do feel a bit saddened to have forgotten the date so badly," he said. "I am however, delighted to have experienced this."

"I know I must have seen something like that when I was a kid back east," Riley said, still awestruck. "But I sure as hell don't remember it."

"I know I've never seen anything like it," Amos said as he scratched his head. "But there's something about it that kind of catches hold of you."

"I heard it said, when I studied in Edinburgh," Jacob said, "that you will feel it if you carry Scottish blood. You must be part Scottish, Amos."

"I remember my grandmother saying that I was," Amos said with a grin. "I might as well be. I'm part everything else anyway."

"Well, I thought a wolf and a mountain lion were killing each other." Riley chuckled. "It's no wonder he never had to fight the Indians. He just played that thing and scared them so bad that they agreed to go to the reservation so they could be protected by the Army."

Jacob was caught funny. He started laughing and could not stop. "I am a Child of the Mountain," he said between laughs, "and I enjoyed the music. I must be more Scottish than you are." He started laughing again.

Amos started chuckling. "I guess we'll have to add Scotty to your list of names then. Doctor Jacob, Scotty, Frenchy, Artemis D'Artagnan, Rides Horse, Long Lost and Then Returned Son of the Chief Hanley."

"Maybe ye should just call him Jake," Mac said as he came out of the door. "By the time ye call him all those other things he will be dead of old age. Ye will need a twenty mule team to drag in a big enough head stone to let the world know who is buried there." He laughed as he sat down on the steps of the porch.

The man with the potentially very long name said hastily, "I'll settle for Jacob."

"Lads, I do this several times a year because I do not want my wee little ones to forget where we came from," Mac said serious-ly. "Nor do I want them to forget the freedom that we did nay have there, but now enjoy so much. Today, I play my pipes to remind them of the grace that has delivered us here." He rose. "On this day we do no work, but spend the whole day telling our children of the old country and of our new country. We want them to be as thankful as their mother and I. Since I have long considered ye to be part of my family, I am proud to be able to share a part of this day with ye." He went back in the house.

"I think I just started liking the music better," Riley said as the three of them took their horses to the barn and put them away. As usual they threw their bedrolls in the loft of the barn. They were not about to let Mac work on their horses, so Amos and Riley made sure that all farrier work was complete before they walked out of the barn. It was a warm day for spring, far warmer than it had been on Laramie Peak. The three were sitting in the shade of the porch, chewing hard tack and sipping water from their canteens.

"What in the world are ye doing?" Missus stood over them with her hands on her hips. "Put that away! I have spent the pre-vious three days making special food from the old country just for this occasion. I'll not have ye ruining your appetites with that nasty old hardtack! Now get cleaned up. Dinner will be served in about an hour!" Orders had been issued and not one of the three grown men was going to argue with her.

They walked back to the barn to wash up. "My brothers," Jacob said very seriously, "I am quite sure I know what she has made. Trust me that it will probably be delicious. However, under no circumstances are you to ask her what is in it. Doing so could cause serious embarrassment to all of us." Riley started to say something but Jacob held up his hand to stop him. "Under no circumstances!" Jacob said in a very firm voice. "Someday I will explain it to you."

As Jacob had predicted, the meal was excellent. The main course was a dish, called haggis, which Amos had never eaten. It was a bit like sausage, somewhat spicy, and yet had oatmeal, some sort of meat and other vegetables with it. There were other vegetables served on the side and a delicious oatmeal bread to go with it and of course some very good coffee. Dessert was a different spicy oatmeal bread with cream and wild berries. It was also delicious. Amos noticed Riley looking at the main course and occasionally poking at it with his fork. He did not, however, ask anything about it and he ate plenty of it. Later in the evening, after the children had gone to bed Mac got out the "good stuff" and offered a toast of thanks for friends and family.

They slept that night in the barn loft. The night was cool, as spring nights usually are in Wyoming, but the ever present heat from the forge kept the chill off and made for very pleasant sleeping. The next morning they rose and had breakfast with their friends before heading on to Medicine Bow. They took the back way, mostly because it was shorter and a more peaceful ride. They rode up to the TIC office building and went in to report to Ted Brow.

"I know you three from somewhere," he said and chuckled. "If you're looking for work, we're fresh out." He chuckled again. "It's about time you characters got back. We've got a big round up going on this spring and we're starting to need a little bit of help." He sat back in his chair. "I've got a couple of things before I forget. Marshall Hanley wants to talk to you three sometime in the next few weeks, and Ned Hogan sent a couple of hundred dollars for you guys to the bank in Laramie and Cullen has matched it. I still want to hear how all that worked out," the TIC agent said as he cocked his head and looked at them. "It doesn't look like you starved to death while you were up there." He chuckled again.

"No, we didn't," Riley said as he grinned and patted his belly. "And we didn't have to take so much abuse either."

Ted Brow actually laughed out loud. "Well, the abuse is just about to start," he said sarcastically. "I was going to give you a little time off for a day or two, but it looks like you've been on about a month's worth a vacation already. Why don't you go ahead and ride on over to Carbon? I'm pretty sure Clancy can find something to do with you." They heard him chuckle again as they went out the door.

CHAPTER 10

DIGNITY (1878)

It was a typical late April afternoon; the sun would come out and the jackets would come off and five minutes later it would get cloudy, or the breeze would come up and the jackets would be put back on. All in all, it was a very beautiful spring day. They arrived at the Carbon Ranch house a couple of hours before the crew was due to get back in. Amos talked old Charlie the cook out of a cup of coffee, however the famous fruit upside-down cake was not yet done. The coffee was good, but did not compare to what Mother Hogan had made.

Clancy and the crew came in just as the sun set. He put his horse away and came in. He took one look at the three men sitting at the table and hollered, "Charlie!" The cook looked out the kitchen door. "Are you feeding bums again? I thought I told you not to do that, especially the ones that we can't get any work out of," he said as he laughed and extended his hand to each of them. "Good to have you back," he said as he sat down with them. "You're just in time. We have a lot of new calves, and the herd is spread out. I could use you guys up along the north end and over towards the Foote Creek Rim." They each nodded to him.

"Jacob, I haven't been able to check on your people for a while," Clancy said as he gestured roughly south. "Why don't you go up to the White Rocks and see if they're alright?" Clancy thought for a minute. "Be sure to take some salt and dried apples. If everything is okay, then you can swing over to the upper place and help MacGill and his crew out. Take an extra pack horse, you might need to get them a deer or an elk or something," Clancy said with a smile.

"I would like that," Jacob replied. "Thank you."

"You can head out in the morning. In the meantime I'll try to teach these two what a cow looks like," Clancy said and chuckled.

"In the last month I think I found out more about what cows, and every other form of critter look like on the inside than I ever wanted to know," Riley said as he rolled his eyes. "You can't believe the bone piles we found."

Amos ate supper with the crew, then related the story of what had happened at the Laramie Peak Ranch. The rest of the hands sat around the table sipping coffee and listening to him. Even Charlie came in and sat for a while. When the story was done there were a number of men who found the tale amazing, while others shook their heads and made reference to old mountain man stories.

"Okay, all you nonbelievers," Riley said and pointed a finger in the air. "You sit right there for a minute." He got up and went outside for a couple of minutes. He returned carrying something rolled up in a blanket. He set it on the table and unrolled it. Inside was the largest mountain lion skull that any of them had ever seen. When the oohs and awes stopped he finished unrolling the blanket. Inside was a grizzly bear skull that was well over a foot and a half long, and it had the lower jaw with it. The cowboys stared at the skull and at the fangs that were more than four inches long.

"I ain't never seen one that big!" one of them said. "Hate like hell to have that one bite me." That seemed to be the general consensus.

"There was this one, and another one that was almost as big," Riley said. "I suspect that if I had wanted to dig around there would've been several more." Any doubt of what they had done seemed to be gone.

"I think I'll get me one of them that's still alive," Clancy said and chuckled. "That way I won't ever have to chew anybody's ass out again. I'll just turn it over to the bear." Everyone laughed and two or three said "ouch" as they headed for the bunkhouse.

"I did not know that you had those," Jacob said has he helped Riley roll up the skulls in the blanket. "What do you intend to do with them?"

Jacob started to speak but Amos interrupted him. "I figure the 'old mountain man' here, will keep them around to show off when he tells everyone how he killed them both with a pocketknife," Amos said as he began laughing. "He'll probably say that he got them both at the same time, one in each hand, and he was saving Jim Bridger's life at the time." Riley rolled his eyes and scowled at Amos.

Jacob did not crack a smile. "We Indians would probably have used a willow switch," he said flatly. "The question remains however, what do you intend to do with these treasures."

Riley started towards the bunkhouse. "Me and old Jim couldn't find any willows way up on that mountain so we used our bare hands." He tried to sound very casual. He waited for a few seconds, but did not get a response from either of his friends. "I really don't know," Riley said. "I'm afraid they'll just get broken up here. I kind of thought about sending them back east to my family, but I really don't think they would find them all that interesting."

"If I could make a suggestion," Jacob said as he stopped walking. "I do not mean to sound selfish, however Mr. Hanley, my adoptive father, would greatly treasure them. If you…." He started to say more but Riley jumped right in.

"Hell, yeah! That's a great idea!" Riley said. "He's done so much to help me with the horses. The least I can do is send him a couple of old skulls!" He started to hand them to Jacob. "You know more about sending samples and rocks and things back east than I do. You figure out how to get them there, and I'll be happy to pay the shipping." Riley started walking again. "Damn, I'm sure glad I…I mean you thought of that." Jacob looked at Amos, shrugged, and followed after Riley.

The next morning they explained what they planned to Clancy and asked him to keep the skulls in his office for safety. He liked the idea and immediately agreed. Amos and Riley went out a little bit early to configure their gear to be cowboys again, instead of travelers. Jacob had little to do since his horse and pack horse would not need to be changed. The two pack horses that Riley and Amos had used were already fitted and ready to go, so Jacob took both of them.

Riley, Amos and the rest of the crew were already gone before Jacob headed south. Amos now had a pretty good idea of what he was doing as a cowboy, but he could not help remembering the day he had first met Riley. Today there were more and probably better cattle than there had been eight years earlier. It had been then that he had done some trading with Riley to get the saddle he was now riding. "How much better I've got it now," he said to himself as he thought about the old army saddle he had been riding. It was still in the tack shed at the Carbon Ranch where he had left it. He had never gotten around to taking it to Tom Sherman Junior in Medicine Bow.

The way they went, they were practically back to Medicine Bow before they started to swing toward Foote Creek Rim. They had already found a number of cattle that needed to be moved upstream to the south along the Medicine Bow River. No one had said anything about missing horses, but on the flat between Iron Hill and Indian Hill they discovered the tracks of about twenty horses headed southeast. The tracks had not been there two days before when they came from Mac's place on Rock River to Medicine Bow. Only three horses were shod, and that pretty much meant that the rest were stolen. They decided to split up, Riley would continue moving the cattle while Amos would follow the tracks. He went far enough to know that the horses had not gone toward Mac's place but had gone upstream and were probably going southward along the east side of the Medicine Bow Mountains.

The problem was that he did not know whose horses they were, or whether they were actually stolen. In any event, he did not have the right gear to go after them and he did not want to leave Riley wondering what had happened. Amos got out his spyglass and scanned the area for a few minutes but could see nothing. With two days head start in the rolling foothills of the mountains, it was unlikely that he would see them. He made a few mental notes, then hurried back to catch up with Riley.

They got back to the ranch house later than the rest of the crew, but Charlie had kept a couple of plates of food for them.

Amos related what they had seen and Clancy immediately went to send a telegram to Ted Brow. In a few minutes he came back. "Ted is not aware that we're missing anything," Clancy said. "But a couple of men from one of the outfits over towards the Shirley Mountains came through today missing about twenty head. He wants us to check our horses out and get back to him. Right now he doesn't want to take the time to work on someone else's problem."

"I'll get up a little bit early then," Riley said shaking his head. He was obviously aggravated. "And go walk around the corrals. When we ride out we'll get everybody to look for unshod horse tracks. I sure hope they didn't get one of those good mares that I've been trying to build up a bloodline with."

The next day Riley got up early, walked around the corrals, and looked at the horses. Amos got up at the same time and saddled Riley's horse for him. Over breakfast Riley told Clancy that they might be missing two horses, but they were not the best ones and they could easily have gone to the upper ranch. He wrote down a brief description that could be sent along with the freight wagon that was going there anyway. Much to Riley's relief, the two horses were at the upper ranch house.

April rolled into May, and eventually, May began to approach June. The spring roundup had gone off quite well and the TIC ranch was in excellent shape after the winter. The cattle had been pushed up the Medicine Bow River as far as they were going to be until the high snow came off and all the marking and branding was done. The upper and lower ranch crews were working as one when Amos and Riley finally happened to bump into Jacob. The first thing Amos asked was about the welfare of the Children of the Mountain. Jacob said that they were doing all right, but it was obvious to see that he was deeply concerned. Amos finally got him to talk about it.

"Health and provision wise, they are doing quite well," Jacob said as he stared at the ground but was really looking at noth-ing. "What I am very deeply concerned with, is that there are only seven of them left. Three of them are almost beyond their… uh…reproductive years and the four younger ones are brothers and sisters. I really don't see how the group can be sustained for another generation." He looked up at his friends as the tears edged his eyes. "Moreover, I do not know all the stories and legends that I would have learned had I grown up with them. There is no written language and I'm afraid that the oral language will be lost forever." He was quiet for a minute. "I can see that I am feeling sorry for myself and I do not mean to," he said as he wiped his cheek. "Forgive me for being so undignified about this." He paused again. "Believe me I am grateful to have my two brothers here to talk about it with."

"Jacob," Riley said softly as he stepped forward and put his arm around his brother's shoulders. "Dignity ain't got a damn thing to do with it."

CHAPTER 11

CHAIN GANG (1878)

Marking and branding the cattle was pretty much under control by the first week of June. The Children of the Mountain had left the White Rocks that were their winter quarters, and Jacob had taken his prospecting equipment and gone looking for precious metals. Amos and Riley had spent several days with him and had done all they could, but they knew that Jacob had to work through things by himself and the high mountains were the best place to do it.

A telegram came asking Amos and Riley to join Marshall Hanley and a number of other men in Laramie one week later. Since there was plenty of time and they were already at the Upper River Ranch house, they decided to ride around the end of the mountain on the old Overland Stage route and then go into Laramie. With a week to travel, ten or fifteen miles a day would make an easy trip. The first night they camped in the upper end of Rock Creek, where they were able to catch several good trout for their evening meal. The second night they found a nice little meadow near where the several forks of Mill Creek came together. Again there was trout for supper. This time Riley did the fishing while Amos did the cleaning and got the fish ready to cook.

They had thought to stop and visit MaryKathleen and were nearing the crossing of the Little Laramie River on the wagon road between Laramie and Centennial. As they approached a man stood up waved his arms weakly, staggered forward and fell into the river. Although not impossible to cross, it was still running high water and whoever it was began to wash downstream. Amos and Riley galloped to the streamside and waded in. It was a good thing that there were two of them, because the current was moving its victim quickly downstream and it was unlikely that one man could have stood against it. Waist deep in cold water, they managed to flip him over so he could be face up. Amos was shocked to see Patches Johansen coughing and spitting out water. They drug him onto a gravel bar beside the stream, sat him up and pounded his back while he got breathing again. It was obvious that he was pretty beat up, and it was not just from his fall in the river.

"Riley, Riley is that you?" The old mountain man could barely see through his swollen eyes. "Old son," he sputtered and caught his breath. "You don't know how powerful glad this old child is to see you!" He rested for a moment. "Them two bastards worked me over and took my horses. I was afraid they was gonna do me in. I eased off and hid all night, then the next day I was pretty sure they was gone so I started walking. You know, I aint quite as strong as I used to be." He chuckled weakly. "I do believe that old man river might have taken me if you boys hadn't happened along."

"Who got your horses Patches?" Riley asked, still holding him up in a sitting position.

"A couple of Earl Simmons' boys," the old man said and tried to stand up. Riley convinced him to rest for a few more minutes. "I was just gittin' back from Laramie and they must have been there watchin', cause they waited till I was all unhitched 'fore they jumped me." He closed his eyes for a minute, and then looked up again. "You know, that one son of a bitch said he wanted to burn my wagon! He said it smelled bad! Hadn't been for that other son of a bitch my wagon would be gone too. He said a fire might attract too much attention. Imagine that, stealing a man's horses, beatin' the hell out of him, and then insultin' his wagon!" Patches said sadly. "Things sure aint like they used to be."

The old man was getting pretty weak. Amos made a place in the grass for him to rest. Riley helped him over and he was asleep almost immediately. "What are we going to do now?" Riley asked as he put a blanket over the mountain man.

"I'll tell you what we're going to do!" Amos said. He was more than mad. "You take care of him and I'll head to Fort Sanders to get some help. If everything goes right I should be back here late tomorrow with a wagon and maybe some medical help. The next day we can get him to the fort. After that I'm going to find the bastards that did this to him and kill both of them!"

"Amos," Riley said holding up his hands. "You might need to calm down a little. If you go riding in to a bunch of horse thieves, guns blazing and fire in your eyes, you're probably the one that's going to get killed."

"I didn't mean that I have to do it right now," Amos said, still fuming. "What I'm saying is that sooner or later we're going to bump into those bastards. With what we're doing we can't hardly help but run into them." A look of pain crossed Amos's face. "I just can't let somebody like that beat up on women, kids, or old fellas like him, I just can't!"

Amos got his slicker from his pack horse and tied it on his saddle, then put a handful of jerky in his saddlebag. He left his rifles with Riley, climbed on Daniel and trotted east. It was over twenty miles to Fort Sanders and they covered it in four hours. They stopped only where there was water for Daniel to drink while Amos chewed some jerky and got a quick drink from his canteen. At the fort he went directly to the Commanding Officer's quarters. The Colonel commanding Fort Sanders was immediately angered by what had happened and called for an ambulance and driver along with a detachment of six cavalry men to start immediately toward Centennial. Everyone knew Patches and liked the old man. More than twenty troopers and both field surgeons quickly volunteered for the eight positions. Amos could have stayed at the fort, but chose to stable Daniel and ride along on the ambulance. It was well after dark when they stopped for the night. They were already over halfway back and would easily be there in the morning. Talk beside the campfire revolved around the hope that they would catch the offending horse thieves, and the frontier justice that would be administered to them.

The sky was only gray when they arose, and the first colors of sunrise were just beginning to show over the Laramie Mountains when they got underway. Breakfast had been warm coffee, left-over from the night before, and a handful of hardtack. They moved along quickly and the pounding of the ambulance made Amos appreciate Daniel all the more. When they were within two miles of the river crossing a pair of troopers galloped on ahead to let Riley know they were coming. The ambulance driver must've been an old hand at what he was doing because he barely slowed his four horse hitch when they crossed the river. He brought the ambulance to a halt a few yards from where the old man lay in the grass.

Amos jumped from the ambulance and ran over. "How's he doing?" he asked. Patches smiled up at him.

"I think he'll be okay," Riley said as he helped the old man with a cup of coffee. "I sure wish Jacob was here, he knows a lot more about this than I do. I think the old fella has got a couple of broken bones, one on his right leg and the other one on his right arm. There's a pretty good knot on his head too, but that's been going down overnight."

"Damn right I'll be okay!" Patches said over the top of his coffee cup. "This aint near as bad as when that old she bear got me. I got meat to deliver! People are countin' on me!"

A few minutes later the field surgeon confirmed that the right arm was cracked, but not broken and the right leg was bruised but otherwise all right. The bump on the head would probably go down. "That is one tough old kid," the surgeon said. "Not many people his age could walk as far as he did, even if they weren't hurt."

Amos let out a deep sigh of relief. "Come on," he said to Riley. "I'll help you get packed up. I've got to tell you, I'd a lot rather be riding a horse than banging along in that ambulance." By the time they got packed up the field surgeon had treated Patches and he had been made comfortable on a large pile of pads and blankets in the ambulance. Every trooper came over to wish him well. It was still only nine o'clock in the morning, but the trip back to the fort would be necessarily slow. It would probably be near dark, or later by the time they got there.

When they finally rumbled into the fort Amos had a serious pain in his backside, and Riley had a serious grin about it. Amos hobbled into the Colonel's office; the evening meal was over, but the mess hall had kept plenty of food warm for the incoming troopers. Amos was tired; the past couple of days have been both physically demanding and mentally stressful. Before eating he and Riley wanted to make their report to the Commanding Officer and to thank him for his help. Everything Amos had to say was in support of what all the troopers had said or what Riley had told them about finding Patches Johanson.

The Colonel nodded. "Mister Moss, as far as I can see, you and Mister O'Riley did everything that could possibly be asked of either a civilian or of military personnel," he said.

"Colonel," Amos asked. "I have to ask you why you have so much concern for old Patches?"

"He kept this fort supplied with meat for all these years, especially the early years," the Post Commander replied, smiling slightly. "Through raging blizzards and stifling heat we could always count on him. He unquestionably saved a goodly number of people from going hungry here. The least we can do is to help him in this time of need." He thought for a moment. "One last thing, Mister Moss," he stepped close to Amos and his voice was barely a whisper. "Between you and me and off the record, should the men who have done this happen to become deceased, I am quite sure that any ruling coming from this office will show that it was self-defense or accidental, possibly even suicide. The Colonel smiled briefly and nodded.

Amos looked at the officer for a few seconds, then smiled very slightly and nodded back. Just then there was a knock at the door and Corporal Webber came in with his usual handful of papers. "Sheriff Tower is here to see you Sir," he said and saluted, papers still in hand.

Nathan was shown in. "I understand you have arrested this miscreant and his accomplice," he said in his most monotone voice. "I'm here to transport them to the local restaurant where they will be punished by having to eat the best steaks in the house." The solemn mood that Amos had known for two days was broken.

"Yes indeed," the Colonel laughed. "While you're at it, force them to drink a couple of beers on me." He took a dollar from his pocket and flipped it to Nathan.

Nathan saluted. "Punishment will be carried out immediately Sir," he said trying not to laugh. As Amos turned to look at the Colonel, Nathan put a single handcuff on his wrist and put the other side around his own. Amos's eyes were wide. "Stop trying to resist or I'll be forced to put you up at the hotel for the night." Nathan's voice was still dead flat.

The Colonel was sitting in his chair laughing and pointing at Amos. "You should see your face," he said and began laughing again. Amos hung his head and shuffled out the door as if he were on the chain gang.

Outside there was a buckboard and Riley was waiting for them. Amos put his hand out to have the handcuffs taken off since the prank was over. Nathan looked him square in the eye. "I take it you thought I was kidding," Nathan said as he took the handcuff off of his own wrist and climbed in. Riley pointed at Amos and started to laugh only to have Nathan whip the handcuff on him. It was now Amos's turn to laugh. Nathan slid into the driver's seat and transported his newly acquired chain gang to the restaurant.

CHAPTER 12

LOST JACKET (1878)

Nathan left the handcuffs on during the drive back to town. When they arrived at the restaurant Amos had expected him to take them off. Instead, he said, "I've got an idea for a good joke." He chuckled. "Just play along for a few minutes, this should be good." They got down from the buckboard, but Nathan had them wait outside for a minute. He went in and, in his most monotone voice, called to his wife, "Mary Beth, I've got two prisoners here to feed, come on out for a minute." She came from the kitchen, wiping her hands on her apron. Nathan stepped to the door and motioned to Amos and Riley to step in. Her jaw dropped for a second, and then she figured out what was going on and scowled at Nathan. "Two of the best steaks you have," he said and finally cracked a smile. "These two just saved old Patches Johanson's life." He took the handcuffs off.

Mary Beth placed the order, then came back and had to hear the story. Riley related it to her. "When he's up and around," she said seriously, "you guys bring him in here and I'm going to feed him the best steak he ever had. If it wasn't for him this restaurant would never have been able to be in business, especially in the first few years." She smiled at Nathan. "I guess you could say, that if it wasn't for Patches, we would never have met and we wouldn't have our children." She smiled again.

"Children?" Riley asked. "As in more than one?"

She smiled and laid her hand on her stomach. "I think you un-cles should start making plans to come back here for Christmas and don't forget Jacob." She headed back towards the kitchen.

Riley and Amos both lowered their heads and looked through their eyebrows at Nathan. "Well, I was going to tell you," his face reddened as he spoke. "You know how it is."

"I don't," Amos said and shrugged. "But I'm sure Papa O'Riley here will tell me all about it." If looks could kill Amos would already have been buried. Fortunately the steaks arrived quickly. They were large, thick, and delicious and were from the buffalo old Patches had brought in only a few days earlier. There were not many buffalo left around, and Mary Beth intended to save one of the best steaks for the old man.

When the meal was eaten, Mary Beth brought in desert. Amos had just finished the steak along with his last sip of coffee, when she brought in a mug of cold beer. He didn't think he could hold it, but after the first sip he changed his mind. "Nathan," Amos asked quietly as he stared at the mug. "What do you know about these horse thieves and the posse that is being put together to chase them?"

Nathan thought for a minute, and let out a deep sigh. "Well," he said, "I'm not supposed to say anything, but you'll be hearing it in a day or so anyway. Just don't let it out too early." They both nod-ded. He spoke quietly, "The Wyoming Stock Growers Association is going to send Billy Lykins after them. Doc Middleton steals from everyone and blames the Indians and then when he steals from the Indians he blames the settlers. If it doesn't get straightened out there's going to be some pretty sizable problems." He paused for a moment. "There're a pretty good chance that some of the rustlers and horse thieves you've been after, including the ones that got Patches, are riding with him."

"Do you know who got Patches?" Amos asked. Riley could see the same anger building up again.

"I don't have a clue," Nathan said as he shook his head and shrugged. "I do have something that you're going find amazing though. In a couple of days, when old Patches is feeling up to it, I have someone who can draw a portrait pretty well just by the description of the man. We could take him out to the fort and have him sit with Patches and make up a picture. If we do that I might be able to tell you who it is from the wanted posters down at the office."

"Who the heck would that be?" Riley asked.

"As I understand it," Nathan said trying not to laugh, "he's a close associate and partner in crime of yours." Nathan looked at Riley and grinned. "Olaf Nordquist," Nathan said as he cracked up and a couple of seconds later Amos did too. Poor Riley's face fell; once again he was the butt of a joke he had not started, or probably ever been part of and was powerless to stop. He just sat looking at his beer and waiting until the laughter died down.

Amos had totally forgotten, but now it made perfect sense to him. Olaf had been drawing animals, scenery and portraits of the people around him for many years. He had a little tablet of paper and a few pencils that he took with him almost everywhere. Amos had watched him draw a remarkable picture of his own horse as they sat overlooking the North Platte River years before.

Riley looked around the table. "I'm going to shoot the first guy," he said with a deep sigh, "that says the word Papa." The laughter started again and Amos was glad. He needed something to break the malevolent mood he had been in, and this evening was it.

"The meeting is the day after tomorrow," Nathan said. "Let's have breakfast in the morning, and then go out to the fort. I'll round up Olaf; tomorrow is his day off anyway, and we can give him a couple of dollars to go out and draw pictures. I'm sure he will be very happy to do it." Nathan cracked a smile again and said, "I'm not sure we should take Riley you know, competitive spirit and all that sort of thing. Then again, maybe we should keep an eye on him." Riley scowled and pretended to reach for his gun.

Nathan walked them back to the hotel and then headed back to the restaurant. He would wait for Mary Beth to get done and drive her home. When they got to the top of the stairs Amos stopped. "Riley," he said as he looked around the stairs but was not really looking at anything, "I know you're right about me getting mad, and I guess you know the reasons why. I know you took a lot of crap tonight, but you also got me thinking straight again and I just want to thank you. Just one question though," Amos said and cocked his head to look sideways at Riley. "Was Nathan in on this, or did it just happen?"

Riley was just entering his room. He looked over his shoulder. "As Jacob would say in the language of his people," Riley said as he flashed his usual grin, "Yes."

Amos slept well but woke early and lay in bed trying to see the faces of everyone he had seen who had been involved in rustling and horse thievery. He finally gave up, got out of bed and got dressed. He sat in a chair trying to put two and two together but came to no conclusions. At seven o'clock he went to the restaurant for breakfast. He was much too early and sat at the usual table with his back to the wall while he thought over the events of the last few days. He saw Riley walk up and they were soon joined by Nathan and Olaf Nordquist. Three of the men were not particularly hungry and ordered biscuits and gravy. Olaf seemed to be starving, and was thrilled to death to be getting to eat in a restaurant, especially when they offered to buy him steak and eggs.

There was some talk about Olaf's new baby and the one that was due soon. Riley managed to change the subject as often as possible and became very interested in Olaf's art work. Olaf was, of course, very happy to have anyone interested in what he was doing and brought out several sketch pads of what he had drawn. They were remarkably good and Nathan bought one of his wife and their first baby. He said he intended to get it framed. Amos put it in the back of his mind to have a portrait drawn of himself, Riley and Jacob the next time they were in town together.

With breakfast over, they all got in the buckboard and Nathan drove them to Fort Sanders. The first thing Amos did was to go to the surgeon's office and inquire about Patches Johanson. "Tell me, Doctor," he said as he looked straight at the surgeon. "And please tell me the real story; how is the old man?"

"In all honesty," the Doctor said, "that old coot is doing much better than I thought he would. I don't know how old he is, but he has to be near seventy. He says he's a hundred and thirty." They both laughed. "Somehow I doubt that. The way he's recovering would match someone around forty. You can go to the infirmary and see him if you wish. Oh, and by the way," the Doctor said,

"I convinced him that I needed to put him under to fix his arm, which was in a way true. However, while he was under we took the opportunity to do some very serious cleaning. He was thrilled to death to have new clothes, but wants his old jacket back. It's hanging outside and downwind." They both laughed again. "He's been badgering everybody to get him a drink. It wouldn't really hurt him." the doctor said and got a small bottle from his desk. "Give him this, it's pretty watered down. It's more flavor than anything, and it might help keep him thinking about the pictures."

Amos went to the dispensary and found that Nathan, Riley and Olaf were already there. Patches was in his height of glory explaining, in much embellished terms, how he had fought the thieves nearly to death before they managed to get the jump on him. The story was somewhat different than it had been on the riverbank. When the tale slowed down, they got him to describe his ambushers as best he could. For well over two hours, Olaf drew, erased and drew again. Finally Patches was happy with the pictures. Between drawings the old man had managed to drink the whole bottle Amos had brought him. "Don't have near as much bite to it as the stuff back at camp," he said as he drained the last of the bottle. "But it beats the hell out of that stuff they call water here." Everyone nodded in agreement.

Nathan and Riley looked at the pictures and then at each other, and nodded. "I can tell you exactly who the one is," Riley said. "That's Earl Simmons' younger brother, Newt." Nathan nodded in agreement.

"I can't remember the name of the other one," Nathan said looking at the drawing. "But I know I have a poster on him back at the office." They told Patches about their plans to get him a steak dinner as soon as he was able. They didn't tell him about their plans to lose his jacket and then miraculously find it just as he was leaving town.

They drove back to Nathan's office through a beautiful spring day, though the clouds on the western horizon spoke of possible rain that evening. They left the buckboard at Tom Sherman's stable and walked to the Sheriff's office. Nathan dug out a huge pile of wanted posters. Some were more than two years old. It took several hours to compare the drawings to the posters. Finally, in the very last few they found a match. The poster was more than a year old, but it was unmistakable.

"I guess I might've known," Nathan said. "That's Allen Baldwin, one of the Baldwin brothers that run with Doc Middleton. He's about as crooked a human being as has ever set foot on the earth. He doesn't care who he steals from, or who he leaves in a lurch. He'd shake your hand, stab you in the back, steal your horses and then run off when things got tough. If you bump into him remember that he is as sneaky as they get; keep your eye on him. I'm pretty sure it would be self-defense if you shot him." It was easy to see that Nathan did not like the man in the picture.

CHAPTER 13

NEWT (1878)

The next morning Amos and Riley met with Nathan to have breakfast. Nathan brought along United States Marshall Samuel Hanley and a man introduced as Billy Lykins, who had been appointed by the Wyoming Stock Growers Association to go after Doc Middleton. Neither Lykins nor Hanley wanted to say anything about the upcoming action since they were both well aware that Middleton could have spies anywhere. The actual meeting was to be held in a guarded building outside of town. They finished breakfast and the four of them got in a covered buggy to be driven to the meeting place. Nathan was not to be part of the posse since he had duties in town and Sam Hanley did not want to take a chance on him getting killed since he was married and had a child plus a baby on the way.

All told there were about a dozen men at the meeting. Sam Hanley spoke first and gave the background information on Middleton. Doc Middleton's real name was James Middleton Riley. He had been on the wrong side of the law since he was a boy in Texas. Before he was twenty he had been convicted of murder and sentenced to life in prison in Texas. In short order he escaped and went north to Iowa. There he was captured stealing horses and spent a year and a half in prison. After release he moved on to Nebraska. There he quickly got into an argument with a soldier and shot him. He was captured and jailed but escaped when the Sheriff let him go rather than have the townspeople lynch him. Shortly after that he showed up near Fort Laramie. He formed a gang of horse thieves called the Pony Boys and had been rustling and stealing horses since then. Two of the men known to be in the gang were Johnny Baldwin and Henry Skurry; both were Texans, and thought to be earlier accomplices of Middleton. The gang had worked southeastern Wyoming and northeastern Colorado, along with parts of Kansas and Nebraska. It was estimated that they had stolen over three thousand horses and they were, even now, trailing forty horses that had been stolen in Wyoming to Kansas to be sold.

Earl Simmons and his brother Newt and a number of their men had apparently thrown in with Middleton. They now figured to work a much larger territory, and if they were pursued there would be strength in numbers. There were several instances where the gang had stolen horses in one state and sold them in another, only to have other members of the same gang steal the same horses again and move on to a third state and sometimes even a fourth. They were well organized and Doc Middleton was the mastermind of the entire operation.

Lykins spoke next; he had been made aware just that morning that the stolen horses had been spotted east of Cheyenne the evening before. They were probably being taken to Nebraska or Kansas to be sold. His plan was to take a posse of at least a dozen men on the train to western Nebraska and try to get ahead of Middleton. Saddled horses and provisions were already waiting for them in Cheyenne. Each man was to get his guns and other personal gear and be at the Laramie train depot by eleven that morning. By afternoon, if all went well, they would be into Nebraska and by evening the posse should be ahead of Middleton.

It did not leave a lot of extra time, but at eleven Amos and Riley were at the train depot with their bed rolls, guns and saddle-bags. Each brought their Winchester and Sharps rifles and extra boxes of ammunition for each one. The Winchester ammunition of course also fit their pistols. Amos had more provisions to hunt down a few horse thieves then he'd had for the attack by several hundred Indian warriors on the railroad over a decade before. The men of the posse were spaced out and seated in several different passenger cars. It did not appear that a large group was boarding the train. In Cheyenne they all stayed on the train and watched as eighteen saddled horses were put in stock cars.

"Those look like some pretty nice horses," Riley said casually. Amos just nodded as if he didn't care that much.

Once they left Cheyenne the railroad was headed mostly downhill. The last significant landmarks they saw were a few bluffs in westernmost Nebraska. Amos could not help but remember how the hills of Nebraska had seemed so much larger when he was hunting buffalo with Bill Cody. Now the country looked almost flat to him, especially when compared with the Wind River Mountains or Laramie Peak. Once they hit the flatland he managed to doze off in his seat for a while. It was well into the night when they arrived at Sidney, Nebraska.

Regardless of the hour there was no time to be wasted and Lykins immediately sent out two scouts. They had known they were going and had chosen two very good horses and were riding light. They were away within minutes of the train stopping. The remainder of the group quickly unloaded their gear and fit it to their horses. Riley chose a horse for Amos and one for himself. Amos was more than happy to trust Riley's judgment. They secured their Sharps rifles to the saddle, but tied the Winchesters so they could easily be pulled out with just their right hands, at a full gallop. In thirty minutes the entire group, and several extra horses, was headed south.

The sky was light but the sun had not risen when one of the two scouts came riding in at a gallop and reported. His horse was lathered up and he quickly exchanged it for another. The exhausted horse was left near a small spring where it could feed and rest until he could be picked up when the group came back by. The posse was almost a mile south by the time the scout had switched horses and caught up. Lykins was hot on the trail and nothing was going to deter him from catching the horse thieves. To Amos it was very reminiscent of buffalo hunting. A scout would ride in to report a herd of buffalo and the shooters would thunder out across the plains to intercept them. This time the intended quarry could shoot back.

They rode on until early afternoon when the other scout came in and quietly gathered the men around him. "They're two hills over, along Lodgepole Creek," he whispered. "They're not moving very fast. They probably figure they're safe by now."

Lykins took over and gathered everyone around him; he spoke just loudly enough to be heard. "This is what I want to do," he whispered. "You three men get out east of them." He motioned to the first three men to his left. "You three," he motioned to the three furthest to his right, "get back above them and don't let them head west again. The rest of us are going to go straight over the hill and right at them." He pointed south. "Remember this," he said as he held up his right hand, "the main purpose is to get the horses back, but if you have any question about them surrendering, shoot first and ask questions later. We would like to have Middleton alive if we can." He motioned toward the hill and everybody started riding. Riley had gone with the western group. Amos was with the middle group, which had to wait for a few minutes while the other two groups got into position. He took the opportunity to get his Sharps rifle and shooting sticks out. He loaded the rifle and put a number of the express rounds where he could get to them easily. He also took the leather catch strings from his Winchester and his pistols.

They came over the hill at a full gallop. As soon as they were seen two of the outlaws whirled and galloped away over the hill to the south. Middleton was at the front of the horses and tried to ride south with the other two men. Amos dropped from his horse, cocked his Sharps and fired. Middleton's horse spun and almost went down. Middleton barely managed to stay on as they went over the hill. The rider closest to Lykins put his hands in the air and immediately surrendered. The two men who were bringing up the rear turned and galloped west the way they had come, only to run into Riley and the other two men who were with him. There was gunfire and one of the thieves went down. The other one quickly surrendered and was rapidly handcuffed and tied to his horse. Riley and the other two men quickly rode to join the posse.

"We got em now!" Lykins hollered as he charged up the hill where Middleton had disappeared. On top of the hill there was horsehair and blood and even a patch of leather that must have come from Middleton's saddle. Middleton however had managed to escape. The tracks and the blood trail showed that the horse was severely injured and was getting weaker with each step. In the area just north of the South Platte River there are numerous small hills and gullies. Middleton was able to take advantage of these until he came to the ranch of a man named Smith.

Smith must've been a friend or client of Middleton's, since even though the posse was closing in he sheltered the outlaw and took him to a nearby butte to hide out. The tracks the two left were obvious and holding the high ground was a mistake, for soon most of the posse had surrounded the butte. Shots were exchanged but the men on the butte had only pistols and the range and accuracy of them did not put the posse in much danger.

"Keep em pinned down!" Lykins hollered. The men of the posse opened up even more with their rifles. "You two," he said as he pointed at Amos and Riley, "bring those two canons of yours over here." They quickly joined Lykins behind a rock. "Put a couple of rounds right there by Smith," Lykins said smiling devilishly. "I don't think he has as much stomach for this as Middleton does."

Each of them fired four shots and had started reloading a fifth round when Smith's arm rose above his hiding place waving a white handkerchief. Lykins called for a cease-fire. "Keep your hands in the air and come on down!" he yelled to Smith. Smith rose but Middleton was not to be seen. "Middleton," Lykins' voice carried anger as he cried out, "You can stay up there and you can die, or you can follow Smith down the hill with your arms in the air. The choice is yours, but I'd just about as soon you stayed up there and died." In a few seconds Middleton was following Smith down the hill.

It took only a few minutes to get handcuffs on Smith and Middleton and to securely lash them on horses. "Lykins and I can take these two into Sidney and turn them over to the Sheriff," Hanley said to the posse. "I'm a United States Marshall and that means I have to go with Lykins, since we're not in Wyoming now. What needs to get done is to round up all the horses and get them back to Sidney. The deceased and the horses all need to go to Cheyenne or Laramie. The reward that was offered was done by the Wyoming Stock Growers Association and they need to see the horses and the bodies to pay up." Hanley shrugged. "We're not in a hurry now," he said. "Rest up for a little while and then travel easy; we can go home tomorrow. Put the horses and the deceased on the train that goes to Cheyenne and Laramie. Lykins and I will be a few days, but we'll catch up with you there."

Lykins came over and thanked the group for their help. He was much calmer now, almost like a different person. "This has gone very well," he said and actually smiled for the first time that Amos could remember. "No one was injured and the only casualty was one of the rustlers. Speaking of that, does anyone happen to know who the deceased is?"

"Yeah," Riley said slowly. "That would be Newt Simmons."

CHAPTER 14

ESCAPE (1878)

he horses were held in a loose herd in a bend of Lodgepole Creek. It seemed like there were Lodgepole Creeks and Muddy Creeks and Spring Creeks just about everywhere in the West. This Lodgepole Creek just happened to run toward Julesburg, Colorado. The herd was about twelve miles from Julesburg and thirty miles from Sidney, Nebraska. It was still early enough in the day to make some distance back toward the railroad in Sidney. The herd was moved along easily and allowed to graze and drink all the water they wanted. Near sundown they had made it well more than half way and stopped to make camp. After the hard riding and danger of the day, trailing easily along with the herd of horses was a very relaxing thing to do. Other than a couple of rattlesnakes to deal with, the camp along the creek was pleasant enough. Supper was only hardtack, jerky and water and breakfast would be the same. By rising early and moving along they would be able to catch the train to Laramie the next day.

Amos was glad to have the job nearly over and he was even happier to see that the herd included Patches Johanson's four horse team from his wagon and the saddle horse he used while hunting. Camp that evening was very laid-back, and with as many men as there were, each pair of men only needed to ride nighthawk for about an hour and a half. Riley and Amos drew the last shift of the night. That was both good and bad. They would already be up, dressed and saddled first thing in the morning; on the other hand, they would already be two hours or so into the day when everyone else was fresh. No farther than they had to go it would probably not make much difference.

No one was really put in charge and the men worked well together. Just wanting to be done and headed home was enough incentive for them to get along. When they were a couple of miles from Sidney the two scouts from the day before went on ahead to be sure that pens were ready, and to make arrangements to load about sixty head of horses on the train. When the herd arrived one of the scouts was holding the gate open and the other had gone to a nearby restaurant and ordered sandwiches and coffee for each of the men. The train was due in less than an hour and they wanted to be ready to load quickly.

With almost the entire posse available the loading went very quickly. The saddles and other gear were put in a boxcar and the men all rode in the same passenger car. They were all dusty and were carrying their rifles. They must have looked like a small army going off to war. Unlike troops headed into battle there was no high-spirited enthusiasm, in fact most of the men were asleep by the time the train had made ten miles west. Most of them woke up when the train stopped for fuel and water in Pine Bluffs.

Riley had said very little and seemed to be deep in thought. He stared blankly out the window as they rode along. "You want to tell me about it?" Amos asked him.

"There's not much to tell," Riley said and looked out the window. "Newt and that other guy were riding hell-bent straight at us. One of the guys that was with me yelled at them to stop. The one guy heard him and held up his hands, but Newt just kept on coming." Riley paused and thought for a minute. "I don't know if Newt heard us, but he never drew his guns. Then everybody just started shooting. Hell, he must've been hit six times. I don't know if I hit him or not, but I was shooting," Riley said as he shrugged and looked at the floor. "I know you had it in for him on account of what they did to Patches, but I traded horses with his brother," Riley said with sadness in his voice. "I guess I'm just wondering if he needed to die or not."

A very strong feeling had opened up in Amos. "A few days ago I would've just walked up to him and shot him dead," Amos said as he looked straight at Riley. "Now, for your sake, I guess I would just as soon have caught him and let the law do whatever it wanted with him." They were both silent for a minute. Amos looked at Riley again. "I guess I have to look at it like this," Amos said, tapping his fingers on his knee. "Newt had been a bad man for a long time and he knew what the price could be. If you had caught him, he would be spending a long time in jail or been hanged. I imagine he might rather be dead from a bullet than hung or in prison. I'll tell you this though," Amos said as his voice became hard. "I'd shoot him a hundred times over before I'd let him hurt you or Jacob or Nathan or Patches or Mac or anyone else that's been good to me."

"Well, when you put it that way," Riley said smiling again, "I guess I'm just winding down. And I'm damn glad you didn't get hurt."

"The feeling goes both ways brother," Amos said, smiling at Riley.

The stop in Cheyenne would take over an hour and most of the men went to a nearby restaurant to get something to eat. The horses that the posse had ridden were unloaded along with the stolen horses that were identified as belonging to people in the area. Amos identified the horses that belonged to Patches and they were left on the train along with three that were carrying the TIC brand. Riley was glad to have them back since one was a mare that was important in the line of horses he was trying to establish. When the train finally left for Laramie, Amos and Riley were the only posse members still aboard.

It was approaching midnight when they finally got to Laramie, and it was the wee hours of the morning by the time they took care of the horses, got their gear and made it to the hotel. Fortunately the night clerk at the hotel was a light sleeper; he let them in and they quietly went to their rooms. Even the best coffee in the world would not have kept Amos from going to bed immediately. He dropped his equipment, threw his hat on a chair and kicked off his boots. He lay back on the bed figuring to get undressed in a few minutes. When he woke up to get ready for bed the sun had already come up. By then there wasn't much sense in changing things, so he rolled over and slept until almost eight.

He woke to the sound of Nathan pounding on his door. "Breakfast is waiting on you two," he said in his monotone voice. "If you don't get down here Mary Beth is gonna be taking the edge off of that cleaver of hers on your hide. She just sharpened that cleaver and she gets real mad when someone dulls up her knives." In five minutes Amos had washed, changed his shirt, pulled on his boots, and was headed down the stairs. Riley was two steps ahead of him.

They were exceptionally hungry. Over breakfast they took turns filling in the story of the last few days. When they came to the part about the two men escaping to the south, Nathan looked perturbed. "I would bet you a dollar," he said and frowned, "that those two were that no account son of a bitch Johnny Baldwin, and his worthless partner Henry Skurry. Neither one of them would stand and fight. Like I said, they'll leave anybody in the lurch. It's too bad you didn't shoot the both of them dead." There was a deep-seated anger in Nathan's voice.

"Stop trying to take it easy on them," Riley said, smiling. "Just say it like you mean it."

"I was trying to go easy on your delicate and sensitive ears." Nathan was into his monotone voice again. "So what are you two up to today?"

"I thought we'd go look in on Patches," Amos said. "If he's ready to go I thought we'd bring him in for a good steak dinner."

"Well, you're a little late for that," Nathan said and shrugged. "We had him in here yesterday. That old son of a gun must have eaten half of a buffalo."

"I figured that might be the case," Riley said and chuckled. "He would have drank half of a barrel of whiskey too, if you would've had it for him." They all laughed.

"The surgeon says he can go back to his camp whenever he wants to," Nathan said. "I understand you got his horses back so there wouldn't be any reason not to head that way tomorrow."

"I guess we'll have to round up a saddle for him," Amos said as he was thinking about where to get one. "And a bridle too."

Riley laughed. "That old kid can ride better bareback and sitting backwards than you and I put together can ride in a saddle!" Riley said with a smile. "All we need to do is get him a blanket and a few feet of soft rope and that pony of his will take him home quicker than you and I can get there."

"I guess that takes care of that problem then," Amos said. "When we get done here, we'll go by and see what Tom Sherman has."

Later that day they went out to the rail yard and got Patches' horses. They took them in to Tom Sherman and had them all fresh shod and picked up a saddle blanket and a few feet of cotton rope before taking them back the Fort. That evening they ate supper with Patches and made plans to ride back to his camp above Centennial. Early the next morning they picked him up. He tied a short length of the soft rope around his horse's jaw, laid the saddle blanket in place and jumped aboard. He whistled to his team, they fell in behind him, and the whole bunch headed west. Even Riley was amazed at how well trained the horses were. He and Amos rode beside Patches. The old man didn't seem to tire and stopped only for a few minutes to let his horses drink. They arrived at his camp by midafternoon, which was a couple of hours earlier than Amos had expected.

They looked around and found most of his gear still there. Apparently the horse thieves had only been interested in the animals. Even his old hat was in the branches of a nearby bush. Jerky and coffee and some dried fruit were good enough for supper. "Usually I would've had some meat to cook over the fire," the old man said apologetically. "Next time you come by I'll try to treat you better. I do have a little bit of this though." He rummaged around behind a tree and came back with a jug. "I been missin' this!" he said with a gleam in his eye. He took several big swallows and offered the jug. Amos was trying to think of a polite way to refuse. Patches started laughing. "Don't worry boy," he said and slapped the side of the jug. "This old child wouldn't pull the same trick on you twice." Amos carefully sniffed the jug, and then took a small sip. It really wasn't half bad, but a little bit went a long ways.

It was nice to be in the mountains again, especially after the nights on the flatlands of Nebraska. Amos slept well and woke to the smell of cooking trout. Patches had already been up and was making sure that his guests were well taken care of. They ate well, but then it was time to head back to Laramie. Sam Hanley and Billy Lykins were due to be back and Amos wanted to talk with the two of them. Besides that he wanted to know what had happened to Middleton.

They rode easily along all that day and by evening had covered the thirty miles to Laramie. They had supper with Nathan and he wanted to be sure they would be there the next day to meet with Lykins and Hanley. "I don't know what's going on," Nathan said over supper. "But the telegram said that they wanted to make very sure you would be here. It's probably something to do with the reward money or returning the horses. Anyhow, the train is due in here at eleven tomorrow, and they want to meet with you in my office at about half past eleven."

They finished the meal, said good night to Nathan, had one drink at the saloon and headed to the hotel. Since the meeting would not be held until almost noon there was no point in getting up early. Even though he was awake at sunup, Amos lay in his bed mulling over everything that had happened. They got up, dressed, had breakfast, and then went to the Sheriff's office at the designated time. Lykins and Hanley arrived precisely on schedule. They had vouchers for payments as deputies and shares in the reward money. There would also be money for each horse that was returned. Amos and Riley declined any share in the money that would have been paid for Patches Johanson's horses and requested that it be given to the old mountain man.

All the accounting was done and the money changed hands. "What's going to happen to Middleton and that rancher that helped him?" Riley asked.

"Well," Hanley winced and said, "they escaped."

90

CHAPTER 15

CINNAMON (1878)

"They what?" Riley almost exploded. "I mean…we went clear over there…I shot a guy and…now!"

"What the hell happened?" Amos's voice dropped as it always did when he was very angry.

"Calm down," Sam Hanley said, trying very hard to control the situation. "Let me tell you what happened." Amos, his jaw clenched, nodded. Riley was still wide-eyed and stiff shouldered. "We took them into Sidney and put them in the jail," Hanley sighed. "That night they escaped some way. We aren't sure what happened. The Sheriff said that Baldwin and Skurry came into town very early in the morning and jumped him, then got Middleton and Smith out. Middleton is known to have a hideout and a woman somewhere up along the Dakota border, so we think they headed north."

"I'm not real sure that the Sheriff wasn't in on it!" Bill Lykins growled and looked straight at them. "He had a welt along his eye, but it didn't look like enough to put him down to me. He claims to have been knocked out the whole time."

"We have absolutely no proof of anything," Hanley said as he sighed again and tossed his hands in resignation. "All we know is that they are gone, and what the Sheriff says is a plausible explanation." He paused for a moment. "You two are probably no more upset about this than I am." Anger touched his voice. "We all put in a lot of hard work on this." He shrugged and then said, "At least we got the horses back, and old Patches is in business again. I just want you to know that I'm sorry it happened."

"You don't have a damn thing to be sorry for Sam," Amos said in a voice that was still low and tense. "We're just going to have to find them again."

"That's exactly what I intend to do!" Lykins had fire in his voice. "I hope I can ask for your help again when I find out where they are." Amos nodded but Riley just shrugged.

"Everything that we say here is absolutely confidential." Hanley was almost whispering. "And it is to go no further than this office." He looked around the office as everyone nodded. "Amos, Riley, I know you two have it in for Allen Baldwin because of what he did to Patches Johanson. I really hope you catch him, but I want him alive if it's at all possible." The Marshall made the statement strongly. "He probably knows where Middleton and Smith went and the sooner I get that information, the sooner we can catch them." Everyone nodded in agreement.

Lykins and Hanley rose to go. They each extended their hands and Lykins said, "You two were about as good a help as I could ask for. I'm really sorry the way this turned out. You can be sure that I will not rest until the job is done." They left the office.

Nathan, Amos and Riley sat in the office saying nothing for several minutes. "Sometimes that's just the way it goes in this business," Nathan said as he looked at the pencil he was twirling in his fingers. He raised his head and looked straight at his two friends. "Those two are very good law men. They did everything right, and you caught Middleton and part of his crew and none of the posse got hurt," he said then paused. "It's just that something went wrong on the other end. I know Billy Lykins and I know he is dog determined to get Middleton. I'd bet a month's pay that he has him found in a year, and has him caught within two years. Remember this too; Smith is now an outlaw and has lost his ranch. That might be punishment enough."

"All things considered," Riley said and sounded dejected, "I think it's time to go play cowboy again for a while." Amos was deep in thought and just nodded. They said their goodbyes to Nathan and went to pick up their horses and gear. Tom Sherman at the livery stable pronounced their horses well shod and ready to travel. They could have ridden back to Centennial and gone around the mountain or just loaded up on the train and gone clear to Carbon. There had been enough excitement to last either one of them for a while. They decided to ride west of Laramie a few miles and then take the old Overland Stage road to the Upper River Ranch. They rode slowly; even so, it was still light when they got to the Little Laramie River. It was high and they decided to camp and wait overnight. Generally the river would be down in the morning because the cold night temperatures would slow the snow melt.

Neither one of them had been in a mood to talk much. Camp was set, but it was just a matter of going through the motions. Hardtack and coffee was good enough for supper. They got the horses settled in for the night, then sat staring into the campfire and sipping coffee. "Amos, are you mad about any of this?" Riley asked.

Amos shook his head. "No, I guess not," he said, then thought for a minute. "It's just that we put in a lot of hard work. Now it looks like it all went for nothing."

"Well," Riley said and smiled faintly, "if we had not agreed to go along, we wouldn't have been there when old Patches fell in the river. He'd have drowned for sure and it might be that no one would ever have found him." He paused for a moment. "It seems like that makes the whole thing worthwhile. Besides, we got one of the guys that beat him up." He paused. "Well, at least somebody did."

"You know, Riley," Amos said and smiled for the first time since they had left Laramie, "I think I'm going to consider that to be good enough." That night Amos slept better than he thought he would.

The next day they rode to the Arlington stage stop on Rock Creek. It took a few minutes, but they caught enough trout for supper. The conversation had grown lighter and the laughter more frequent over the course of the day. The highlight came when Amos stepped out onto a bank to look into a pool for fish and slid down waist deep in the cold water. He could say nothing but, "Whoop- whoop -whoop" while Riley rolled around on the bank laughing. Riley cooked the trout while Amos wrang out of his pants and hung them and his boots on some willows to dry.

The next morning, after Amos had dried out, they rode along towards the Upper River Ranch house. As it worked out, they bumped into MacGill and two of the ranch hands on the old stage road. "Well would you look at that," MacGill said sarcastically. "A couple of saddle tramps comin' along just when I was needin' some help. Come on along boys, there might just be room at the ranch for you." It was good to be back. Less than two weeks had expired since they had left, but it seemed like a lifetime. Ranch stew, passable coffee and good conversation helped finish the winding down process. Of course, they had to relate the story of what had happened to the men, but already it seemed like just a story from a bygone time.

It was still only mid-June and the cattle had been pushed as far up the mountain as was practical. Amos figured that the Children of the Mountain would have already left, but MacGill said that Jacob was with them. Amos worried that something might be wrong. A day later he and Riley rode to the White Rocks. Jacob and his people were indeed there, and were sitting in the sun talking. They all stood up and did the greeting ceremony that the old Chief who had adopted them had taught them years before. Now Riley and Amos had managed to come home twice, in as many days. There was really nothing wrong. The Indians had simply decided that there was going to be one more significant storm before summer came on. It was unlikely that they would be wrong. Riley and Amos had brought two pack horses carrying dried fruit and the usual five pounds of salt. The horses were left with Jacob while Amos and Riley went to a small hill to look for game.

They had been there for about an hour and had spotted a small group of deer. "I'll bet he's right behind us," Riley whispered. "He's probably been there for a good ten minutes." Amos just nodded and kept looking through his spyglass.

"To be more precise it has been fifteen minutes," Jacob said as he feigned exasperation. "You two do to seem to know how to take the fun out of things."

"I seem to recall you telling me to listen like an Indian." Amos tried to sound casual, but destroyed the pretense when he started laughing. "I guess that one kind of backfired on you."

"If you are watching like an Indian then I suppose that you have noticed the small group of deer that is up the mountain a short way," Jacob said, ignoring the laughter as he pointed up the mountain. "I notice that you have your Sharps rifles, and I believe there is more than adequate time to harvest one of them. I also assume you noticed that they are moving down country rather than up and grazing early in the day. That would be one of the signs my people use to predict the weather." He walked back down the hill a few yards and whistled. Shortly his horse came out of the willows and walked up to him. "Shall we then?" he said as he swung into his saddle.

It took less than an hour to get close enough for the Sharps to be in range. In another half hour they had cleaned the deer, lashed it on a pack horse and were headed to the White Rocks. The Children of the Mountain had heard the rifle fire and were eagerly waiting near the mouth of their cave. The deer was brought to them and laid on the ground. The ceremony was performed to thank the mountain for the gift of the deer. As usual, Riley and Amos would be left with the task of making reconciliations with the horse for carrying the deer. The Indians made short work of cutting the animal into portions that they could easily handle and soon it was taken to their cave to be butchered.

That night they had deer ribs roasted over a fire. The Indians would usually use the ribs first before they ate the rest of the deer. There was little meat on them and they would dry up quickly and become unusable. It was not uncommon for the little group to eat all of the ribs from a deer in one sitting. They had warmed the dried apples in their steatite bowls until they were the consistency of applesauce. Riley had brought along a small amount of cinnamon which he sprinkled on his bowl of apples. He offered a small amount to the group. It was passed around and, to Riley's chagrin, pronounced to be inedible.

It was a nice evening and a warm breeze was blowing. Amos figured he would sleep out in the meadow, but Jacob told him that the Children of the Mountain were expecting snow that night. Looking at the nearly clear sky he found it hard to believe. However, he took their advice and put his bedroll under an overhang. In the morning water was dripping off the rocks and there were six inches of heavy wet snow in the meadow. Already the wind was ripping clouds from the peaks of the Snowy Mountains and there were patches of blue sky showing to the west. The Chief of the little group spoke to Jacob and told him that as soon as the ground had dried a little bit they would be headed up the mountain.

That afternoon, he gathered Jacob, Riley and Amos about him and performed the departure ceremony. He thanked them for everything and wished them well. In a few moments the little group had started up the mountain.

CHAPTER 16

GOOD LUCK (1878)

Amos, Jacob and Riley rode easily toward the Upper River Ranch house. As they rode into the yard Amos saw several men stringing what appeared to be another telegraph wire into the house. He looked at Jacob. "What happened?" he asked. "Did the old wire wear out or something?"

"No," Jacob chuckled. "This is a different kind of wire. It's somewhat like the telegraph, but you don't have to be able to interpret Morse code to use it. All you have to do is talk into the device and the person at the other end will hear you and he can talk back. It's akin to having a conversation over the telegraph. When they get it hooked up, I'll show you."

"Seems to me," Riley said as he raised an eyebrow, "that you're going to have to yell awful loud to have someone hear you through a wire clear down to Carbon."

"It's even better than that." Jacob sounded excited about the new device. "You can talk all the way to Medicine Bow. Someday, you will be able to talk all the way across the country."

"Has old Patches been teaching you to tell stories?" Riley asked as he smirked at Jacob. "Not like it matters. After all, it's your story and you can make it as big as you want." Amos didn't say anything, but did chuckle.

"Oh ye of little faith," Jacob said and rolled his eyes.

Amos had not said anything, but had been watching his two friends go back and forth. "Why don't you two make it interesting?"

he asked with a smile. "Jacob says it works and Riley thinks its hot air. How about the loser buys the winner a steak dinner next time we get to Laramie?"

"Agreed!" Jacob said quickly and held his index finger up. "And we can let Amos be the judge! The loser will buy the other two a steak dinner; however the two winners will buy the loser a beer to go with it." Riley already knew that betting against Jacob was poor business, but now he was in too deep to back out.

"Sounds fine to me," Amos chuckled. "I don't see how I can lose."

"Oh hell," was all Riley could say. He was already pretty sure about where part of his pay was going.

That evening they sat having the usual stew with the ranch hands. Every so often a bell would ring and they could hear MacGill talking in his office. A few minutes later it would happen again. Sometimes it would ring twice, sometimes it would ring three times and sometimes it would ring four. Eventually a man wearing a cloth cap came out of the office. "You should be in business now Mister MacGill," he said as he pulled a rag from his pocket and wiped grease off some small tools and then his hands.

MacGill came out of his office. "Hey Cookie," he yelled. "Get this fella a plate of stew. The rest of you guys come on in here, you're not going to believe this thing!" Everyone crowded into the office. "This is called a telephone; let me show you how this works," MacGill said very officially. "You put this here thing on your ear to listen, and you talk into here. To get them to talk to you down country you crank this thing here." He pointed to a small crank on the side of the device. "If you crank it twice and then wait, they pick it up down in Medicine Bow; if you crank it three times they pick it up in Carbon. We only answer it if it rings four times; that's kind of like our code," he said and was very proud of himself. "Here, let me show you." Just as he reached for the crank the telephone rang. MacGill jumped and there were snickers throughout the room. MacGill scowled. He waited until the phone rang four times, then picked up the earpiece and hollered "Hello" into it. Then he turned to the mouthpiece and hollered "Hello" again. There were more chuckles. "Who is this?" He was talking very loud. "Yeah, this is me, yeah, MacGill. Hey Clancy, everybody is standing around here looking at this outfit. Could you just say hello so they can believe this thing?" Clancy had to say hello ten times to ten astonished cowhands. Only Jacob did not feel the need for proof.

MacGill shooed everybody out of his office and most of them went back to the dining room table to talk it over. "That's the damnedest thing…" was said by several of the men. Amos noticed that Jacob wasn't saying much. "You don't seem to be as impressed as everybody else," he said as he turned his head and raised an eyebrow. "I suppose this is something your people have had for years," he said and chuckled.

"I'm actually more impressed by how easy it was to come up with a steak dinner." Jacob said and laughed as Riley frowned. "Now," Jacob said as he grinned at Riley. "Let us get back to the main subject. No, my people are still using sign language. I did, however, know that the device had been invented. A fellow named Bell patented it over a year ago. Mister Cullen became aware of it and asked me and a number of other people to review it. He has now made a significant investment in it. I believe the future for this device far exceeds that of the telegraph," he said, then thought for a minute. He turned to Amos and said, "I suspect that Mister Cullen has invested part of the money you have in his bank in this project."

"Well, I guess it wouldn't be here if you didn't think it was all right," Riley said. "I'm just not real sure I like the idea of Clancy being able to chew me out from down there, when I'm clear up here." They laughed.

"As you both know, Mister Cullen is very progressive, especially when it comes to communication," Jacob said. "The installation of this device here at this ranch is an experiment. The problem with it has been the distance between two units. They are doing tests on various means of neutralizing that problem. It is being done here because the various distances between the several houses are about right for the tests. Also, the remoteness of the area will keep other people from trying to steal the device."

"So we have to watch out for horse thieves and cow thieves and now telephone thieves," Riley said as he shook his head. "All

I ever came out here to do was to be a cowboy." Amos laughed lightly and nodded in agreement.

"I truly believe that this device will someday make talking across town as easy as talking from me to you," Jacob said and shrugged. "If the distance problem can be resolved, then people may even be able to talk across the country and perhaps around the world. By the way," he said trying not to laugh, "Should our first telephone conversation be about steak dinners?"

"Yeah, well," Riley replied, trying to ignore Jacob. "If they ever do away with horses it'll be my time to check out." They all went to the bunkhouse.

Amos tried to sleep that night, but he kept having nightmares of old Patches Johanson floating face down in the river. Each time he and Riley turned the old man over there was a dead blue face staring at him, then he would wake up. Over and over he took the shot that threw Doc Middleton from his horse. Each time he tried to hold the gun just a little bit higher but it wouldn't move. He woke again from the ongoing nightmare just as it was getting light. It was not the first time he had endured the nightmares, but this time it had been very vivid and much worse. He could usually shake off dreams; this time he had not been able to. He lay in his bunk. It was cool in the bunkhouse, but he was sweating. He lay thinking until he heard a few of the cowboys starting to stir, then he got up and dressed as quietly as he could.

Outside there was just a bit of a mist and it was just cold enough that the dampness sharpened his focus. He walked slowly to the main house, went in and talked old Charlie the cook out of an early cup of coffee. By the time everyone came in Amos knew what he had to do. He sat at the end of the table, across from Riley and next to Jacob. They ate breakfast with the rest of the crew, but Amos sat a few minutes longer.

"All right, spill it," Riley looked at him and said as seriously as he could. "Something has been eating on you for a while, and I have a feeling it's pretty serious." Jacob nodded in agreement.

Amos told them about the nightmares he had been having. "We already knew about them," Jacob said as he looked up from his coffee. "We can hear you tossing and turning in your bunk."

Amos smiled slightly and then told them about the subject of his dreams. "I think I need to do something about this, or it's going to eat me up," Amos said while he drummed his fingers on the table. "I'm going to go find Baldwin and anyone else that might be with him. And I'm going to find out were Smith and Middleton went." Amos started to say more but then stopped. Jacob noticed it.

"Amos, I have called you my brother for a long time now," Jacob said as he swirled his coffee. "This time it is meant very seriously. You and I are having a similar experience." Amos raised his eyebrows and looked at him. Jacob's voice held sadness. "You are aware of the situation with the decline in the number of my people," he said and sighed. "My nightmares involve the death of the last of the Children of the Mountain. My father…I'm sorry…our father, once told me that dreams sometimes foretell a possible future and are a warning that allows us to make adjustments that will set things right. Many times I have seen the truth in his words." His dark eyes looked straight at Amos. "I believe that, without knowing it, you feel the dreams are such a warning," he said, then paused for a moment. He still looked straight into Amos's eyes as he said, "Whatever you do, know this; I will support you in any way I can, just as I know you would support me." Riley nodded.

They were quiet for a few minutes. Finally Amos slapped his hand on the table. "I'm not going to ask either one of you to go with me," he said. "In a way, I would just as soon you didn't. I think this is something I need to do for myself."

"Amos," Riley said as he reached across the table and laid his hand over Amos's. "I know what you're saying, but it was never a question of needing to ask."

Amos nodded. "I think I'm going to tell MacGill what I'm up to," he said. "Then I'm going to go down to Medicine Bow and talk to Ted Brow. I'm not just sure what I'm doing, but I'm pretty certain he'll have some good advice." Amos smiled. "He always does."

Amos went in to tell MacGill what was going on. "I can't say as I blame you," the foreman said. "But, I want you to stop at Carbon and tell Clancy about this. It might surprise you what he can come up with when you need help. Besides that, it'll give me a chance to fool around with this new telephone thing." He grinned like a child with a new toy.

Riley and Jacob had already left for the day's work. Amos took the time to thoroughly sort out the gear he thought he would need and to place it on a pack horse. He carefully checked all the shoes and made sure his saddle fit Daniel perfectly. It was almost noon when he was ready to go. The cook brought him a sandwich and a cup of coffee, shook his hand and wished him good luck. It's a funny thing about ranch men; they may not know what one of their own is up to, but they seem to know when to wish him good luck.

CHAPTER 17

SCRUFFY (1878)

A mos was so deep in thought that he barely remembered the ride to Carbon. The obvious key to catching Middleton was to find out where he had gone. There were probably six or eight people who knew that, but most of them were on the run. To the best of his recollection, Amos could not remember meeting anyone from Doc Middleton's gang face to face. Granted, he had run into a number of horse thieves and rustlers, but of the ones he had actually talked to, most had guaranteed they were going to leave the state, or they were dead. If Amos could find just one of the gang and convince him that he too was a horse thief or rustler, then perhaps he would be led to Middleton. The question was how.

The summer days were long, and the sun was still above the horizon when Amos rode in to the Carbon Ranch house. The crew had already come in and eaten when Amos got there. He put his horses away and bummed a cup of coffee from old Charlie the cook. Of course Charlie threw in a dish of his famous, at least famous at the ranch, fruit upside-down cake. Amos ate it, bummed another cup of coffee and went to talk to Clancy.

"MacGill told me what you're up to," Clancy said as he scratched his head and looked at the telephone. "Aint that something? Twenty or thirty minutes worth of telegraph work all got done in two minutes, just by talking!" He leaned back in his chair and looked at

Amos. "I know what MacGill says. Now I want you to tell me how you see it."

Amos spent fifteen or twenty minutes telling Clancy what had happened and how he felt about it. When he was done, Clancy went and got each of them another cup of coffee. He didn't say anything when he came back, but sat stirring his coffee with what Amos was sure was the same old dirty spoon that had been on his desk the first time they'd met. Several times Clancy nodded his head as if he were talking to himself. Finally he said, "It doesn't seem likely to me that Middleton's gang is going to be back together right away. I think that they'll get away from where the posse shot them up and each of them will go off on their own until things cool down," he said and looked toward Amos. He was really looking far away. "I think if I were you, I'd go over north and east of Cheyenne and try to look like an out of work horse thief." He chuckled. "They say it takes a thief to catch a thief. Maybe one of them will catch you and put you to work."

That night Amos did not sleep well again. It was not for having nightmares, but because he could not stop thinking about what had to be done. The next day he rose early enough to eat breakfast with the crew. Then he rode to Medicine Bow. Ted Brow was there in his office, as he almost always was. His "all day" pot of coffee was also there; it had been sitting on the stove since breakfast. Amos took a cup to be polite but a sip of it convinced him that it should be used to kill weeds. He managed to dump most of it back in the pot when Brow left the room. Once he got back they settled down to talk.

"Well, I talked to Clancy and MacGill today," Brow said. "Did you know you can get them both on that thing at the same time?" Amos shook his head no. Brow leaned back in his chair with his hands clasped behind his head. "I tend to agree with Clancy, but I would add a couple of things. First, I would get a couple horses to herd along so it looks like you've got something you want to get rid of. Now, as it works out, old man Elliot from up in Shirley Basin has got a few horses out here in the corral that he's planning to sell. You could buy a couple of those and then turn around and sell them when you don't need them anymore." He took a sip of his coffee. "And then, I would be sure to stop and talk with

Mac. He most always knows who's been moving horses around here." He took another sip of coffee and Amos silently shuttered. "It wouldn't hurt to stop in and see Nathan Tower for a minute; he might have something current that you could use."

Amos went to check on the Elliot horses. The old rancher wasn't around but had left the sale of them up to Tom Sherman Junior at the livery stable. They arrived at a fair price and Tom Junior guaranteed to take them back if Amos could not dispose of them elsewhere. That night Amos ate supper with Ted Brow. He could not help but notice how his limp had increased over the years. It would now be almost impossible for Ted to ride a horse. The next morning Amos again ate with the Medicine Bow manager. "One last thing before you go, Amos," Brow said as he got up and opened a cabinet. He pulled out an old gray colored hat with a hawk feather in it and tossed it to Amos. "That hat of yours is kind of a trademark. Take this and leave yours; it'll be here when you get back. You might think about growing a beard and maybe let your hair grow out, just to make you look different. It seems to me that most rustlers and horse thieves look a little bit on the scruffy side," Brow said as he put Amos's hat away. Amos agreed since he was about due for a haircut anyway.

Amos put halters on the two horses he had bought. For the first day or two he would keep them tied to the pack horse. In a few days they would buddy up and they would be far enough away from home that they would just follow along. Once all the horses were outfitted he headed towards Mac's place. It took a couple of miles to get the pecking order established between the pack horse and the two new horses, but once that was done they traveled along easily. By early afternoon he had made it to the MacTavish blacksmith shop. As usual Mac was in his shop hammering on iron. One of the teamsters who still ran his freight wagon along the Fort Fetterman road was having his team reshod. Mac was nearly done with the third of the four big horses.

"Amos, laddie," he said and grinned as he finished setting the nails in the big horseshoe. "Ye got here just in time." He motioned towards the draft horse. "Ye hold him up and I'll tack shoes on him," he said and laughed loudly as he set about clenching the nails. In a few minutes he had finished rasping the foot and tied the horse out at the hitching rail. "Now then," he said wiping sweat from his brow. "Let's ye and I have a wee spot of refreshment. Missus has cold lemonade, and a break before doing that last horse sounds good to me. That one can sometimes be a wee bit of a handful."

Amos had walked halfway across the yard when the MacTavish children saw him. Sarah Bryn, who was now ten and quickly becoming the image of her mother, ran out and hugged her "Uncle" Amos. On the other hand, the twin boys Archibald and Alexander were nine and miniature images of their father, which meant they could probably have carried Amos off if they wanted to. Three year old Jessie MacKenzie MacTavish ran out as best she could. Amos swept her up in his arms and, with the other children hanging on him carried her towards the porch. Mac's wife hugged Amos and sat everyone down on the porch.

Mac had obviously been busy because there was a patio table and chairs that were fit and finished as beautifully as the rocker he had given Mary Beth Tower. They were however considerably sturdier to accommodate Mac. There was quickly a large pitcher of lemonade and a loaf of spiced oatmeal bread set before them, and almost as quickly it was gone. Amos waited until the children had gone off to play and then explained what he was doing.

"That explains your new headgear then," Mac said with a smile. "As I have said before, Amos, I do nay ask their business, I just put shoes on their horses. However, I would think that if ye were to go east over the mountain and into Horse Creek and follow it along, ye might just bump into the type of people you're looking for. It's not a hard trail, but tis far enough away from Laramie and Cheyenne to be overlooked by the constabulary." He laughed then said, "Perhaps ye should not tell Sheriff Nathan Tower where ye came by that bit of information."

"I imagine he already knows," Amos said as he laughed. "I'll probably be lucky if he doesn't come arrest me for being a horse thief."

Amos went out and helped Mac shoe the last horse. It had a nasty habit of leaning on whoever was shoeing it. Mac had a simple system to cure the problem. He would leave the sharp end of a shoeing rasp sticking out of his belt, then when the horse tried to lean in, it would get jabbed in the ribs. Of course Mac was strong enough to push back. After one or two tries the horse decided that good behavior was less painful than being ornery.

Of course, Amos was not allowed to leave without having dinner with the MacTavish family. The huge blacksmith and his quickly growing boys were eating a deer in just a few days. The boys were old enough to be hunting rabbits, sage hens and other small game on their own. Mac was glad they would soon be old enough to hunt deer and elk on their own. Amos was very full when he went to bed and even more so after breakfast the next morning. He rode along easily until the meal had time to settle. He took two days to get to Laramie.

It was early evening when he left the horses at Tom Sherman Senior's livery stable and went to see Nathan Tower at his office. Usually the Sheriff wasn't very busy at this time of day. However, when Amos came in he found United States Marshall Sam Hanley was there going over a number of papers. Apparently there had been an aborted train robbery near Medicine Bow. The two lawmen were busy but took a minute to hear what Amos was doing. Nathan could be of little help, but Hanley handed him a file full of papers.

"See if there is any of this stuff you can use," he said as he handed the file to Amos. "That has everything I know about the Baldwins, Skurry, Middleton, Simmons and Smith. There might even be some stuff on a few others of his gang in there. Write down anything you want, but I will need that file back in the morning. Be sure nobody else sees it." He went back to working on the papers in front of him.

"I'm sorry I don't have any time right now, Amos," Nathan apologized. "When you get back things will probably have calmed down."

Amos had supper alone that night. The restaurant was not crowded and he was able to read through the file and make notes. On the way to the hotel he stopped back at the Sheriff's office to return the files, only to find Nathan and Sam were both still there.

"I've been thinking about this, Amos," Sam said as he handed a piece of paper to Amos. "If you do find one of the gang, send this message to Laramie." It read, "Mister Sam Croft. I have horses available. How many do you need?" Hanley gave Amos a minute to read it. "Sign it Amos Mason," He said and glanced up for a second. "I will send back a number such as seven and that will indicate the day that I'm going to be there and I will have help. It will be kind of like being back at the WIND Ranch." Sam smiled remembering their first meeting. "Oh, nice hat too," he said sarcastically.

Amos agreed, returned the file and said his goodbyes. He had thought to ask Nathan about Mary Beth and their baby, as well as the one that was on the way. As busy as Nathan was Amos figured that no news was probably good news and he started back to the Hotel. As he walked back to his room Amos could not help thinking about Joe Qualls. His brother, Jim Qualls, had come down from Montana and bought into the Bear Paw Ranch, with some help from Timothy Ivanovich Cullen. According to everything Amos had heard he was doing very well. Eventually he would own it. He decided that once the hunt for Middleton was over he would try to get to Lander and meet Jim Qualls.

CHAPTER 18

HORSE CREEK (1878)

In the morning Amos picked up a few supplies and was soon on his way to Horse Creek. That evening he camped near a beaver dam where the two main forks of the creek joined. In the upper end Horse Creek runs fairly straight, as most mountain streams do. However, once it gets away from the mountains it slows down and meanders slowly across the high plains. In the sixty or so miles that the stream travels east it probably meanders more than twice that distance. In the final thirty five miles it travels to the north before entering the North Platte River. It probably winds around for over sixty miles. Amos thought absently that he could probably throw a bottle in the stream, give it two days head start, and still catch up to it well before it got to the North Platte River.

Amos had moved along slowly, making only fifteen to twenty miles each day. On the evening of the sixth day he came to Hawk Springs and made camp. The fishing had gotten progressively poorer the further downstream he had gone. The water had warmed as it wound its way across the prairie and the quality of the fish was much poorer, so much so that Amos had decided to dine on rabbit that evening. He cooked it on a green willow stick over a fire that was also made of willow. Although he had gathered dry wood, the willow left a slightly oily taste on the rabbit.

He had eaten the back half of the rabbit and was debating eating any more of it when two men rode into camp. Amos did not rise but instead rolled onto his right side. He let his jacket fall back to reveal his pistol. The two rode up in a way that seemed to be a little too friendly; their smiles were obviously forced.

"What you doing out here all by yourself Mister?" the lead man asked. He wore a dark hat and a buckskin leather jacket. His skin had been darkened by the weather, but his beard was blonde.

"Well, right now, I'm just having some rabbit," Amos said as he gestured towards the fire. "I've had about all I want, so you boys are welcome to the rest."

"Those are some nice looking horses you have there, Señor," the second man said. His voice carried an accent. "What are you going to do with them?" He was shorter than the lead man, but considerably stockier. He was dark complected and he wore a high crowned hat with a wide brim. Amos figured he must be Mexican.

"You know, as good as that rabbit smells," the man in the buckskin coat said with a grin, "it just wouldn't be right to take it. Since we're going to take your horses, your guns and your gear, we should at least leave you with your rabbit to eat." He put his hand on the grip of the Colt 45 that hung from his right hip. The second man did the same. "Now, if you will just relieve yourself of that hand gun, we can get on with the business at hand," he said as he motioned for Amos to get up.

Amos shrugged and tossed his pistol a few feet away. He rolled onto his stomach and started to push himself up. As he did the second Schofield came to bear on the would-be thieves. "Your guns come out by your fingertips and go towards the front of your horses." His voice had dropped as his anger rose. "Then you will get off your horses and stand beside them with your hands in the air. Any wrong move will get you both killed." They did as they were told.

"Just who are you Señor?" the shorter man growled.

Amos pointed his pistol directly at his questioner and pulled the trigger. His hat fell away behind him and was now more ventilated than it had been. "I'm the guy that's going to shoot about four inches lower the next time you open your mouth," Amos said flatly, trying to be nonchalant. "You will very carefully drop your gun belts with your left hands." Amos waited while they did as they were told. "Now you go right over there and lie face down on the ground with your arms above your head," Amos said to the shorter man as he used his gun to gesture a few feet away. "And you," he said as he looked at the man in the buckskin jacket, "you lie right over there. If either one of you makes a noise or a wrong move, I'll shoot both of you." In a few minutes he had securely tied both of them with their hands behind their backs, retrieved his gun, and had relieved his captives of the hidden guns and knives they both carried, as well as their jackets. He laid each man back against his saddle and ran a rope from their wrist bindings through the saddle gullet. He then staked the saddles to the ground with twenty feet between them. As an added precaution he picketed their horses away from camp.

Neither of the two had spoken since Amos had shot a hole in his attacker's hat. With everything done Amos finally sat down by the fire and began eating some more of his rabbit. He didn't particularly want it and it didn't taste very good, but he was planting an idea in his captive's heads. As the sun began to set he put a little more wood on the fire and warmed up some coffee. They were too far away to benefit from the warmth, but the smoke was blowing their way. The evening breeze had begun to blow and it was easy to see the two tied men were getting cold.

Amos looked at them. "You boys go ahead and enjoy yourselves tonight," he said and chuckled as he took a sip of coffee. "I'll be riding out of here tomorrow. Thanks to you, I'll have two more horses and some gear to sell."

"You can't just leave us out here to die!" the buckskin jacket man said. "You at least got to cut us loose so we can walk out of here."

Amos acted like he was thinking about it. "No, I don't think so," he said and swirled the coffee in his tin cup. "I tell you what, tomorrow I'll tie you two together back to back. I'm sure you'll figure out a way to hop out." He laughed out loud. "Why don't you tell me your names?" he asked. "I'll write it down on something and leave it in your pocket, that way when they find your bodies they'll know who they're burying." He laughed loudly again.

"The law will catch up with you!" There was panic in the dark man's voice. "When they do Señor, they will hang you for sure!"

"Three things wrong with that friend," Amos said and tried to look evil and sound nonchalant at the same time. "First, the law is already after me, and stealing horses is a hanging offense. They can only hang me once, so killing you isn't going to change anything. Besides, you wouldn't be the first ones I've shot. Second, you two were working on stealing my horses, so I figure the law isn't going to be too upset if they find you dead. And last, by the time anybody finds your two rotted up carcasses, I'll be long gone and there won't be anything to show I did it." Amos laughed out loud. "I'm afraid you're going to have to come up with something better than that."

He let them sit for a long time. It was not at all cold, but the two captives were sitting still. With the night breeze blowing they were soon shivering violently. Amos put on his heavier jacket and began to lay out his bedroll.

"Okay, okay," the buckskin jacket man said through chattering teeth. "We'll give you whatever you want if you let us go! You can keep the horses, the saddles and everything, but just let us walk out of here."

Amos appeared to be thinking it over. "Well, I recall asking you about your names a bit ago," he said and reached in his pocket for a pencil stub and a scrap of paper.

"Okay, okay," the buckskin jacket man said and sighed heavily. "I'm Jim Baldwin and this is Jose Sanchez." The name hit Amos like a thunderbolt. It was about the last thing he had expected to hear from them.

"You related to Johnny and Allen Baldwin?" Amos tried to keep his voice flat. "The two guys that used to ride with Doc Middleton, before he got killed."

"Well, yeah," Baldwin stammered. "They're my older brothers. But Doc aint dead!"

"Well that's good to know," Amos said trying to sound relieved. "I was figuring on joining up with him and then I heard he was dead. Where is he?"

"I don't rightly know," Baldwin said and shrugged the best he could with the ropes. "We was going to try to get a bunch of horses together and run em up to the Black Hills. You know, for the miners and all. I hear part of the gang is up there, and I figured I could find my brothers and we could get in with em."

"Well that's a good start then," Amos said as he got up. "Tell you what I'll do, as a friendly gesture I'm gonna throw your bed rolls around you so you can have a nice warm night's sleep. In the morning we can figure out where we're gonna go from here." Before he went to bed, Amos gathered up all of the assorted guns, unloaded them and tied them tightly together through the trigger guards. The knives he tied together and went to the stream. He appeared to throw them well out into the water, but in fact he had dropped them almost on the shore. Even if one of his captives managed to get free during the night he would have a hard time getting to a weapon. Amos slept with one of his pistols in his hand and the other under the jacket he had rolled up as a pillow.

Getting warm under their bed rolls had obviously made the two men sleepy. In a few minutes they were snoring and Amos took the opportunity to get some sleep himself. Halfway through the night he awoke. One of the two men was still snoring but the other was quiet. "Boy," Amos growled. "you're doing a good job of being quiet. I think you better do a good job of sleeping while you got the chance."

"I'm just trying to get comfortable." It was Baldwin speaking. It had been a good thing, because now he knew that Amos was a light sleeper and was keeping an eye on him.

Color was just lighting the sunrise when Amos got up and re-kindled the fire. After he got the coffee started he went over and untied Sanchez. "Kick your boots off," Amos said as he held one of his pistols in his hand. The Mexican did as he was told. "Now, you've got three minutes to get out there and relieve yourself. I don't figure you'll make it too far without your boots. If you try to run I'll shoot Baldwin here, then I'll come find you and do the same."

Baldwin clenched his teeth as he looked at his companion. Sanchez nodded his head in agreement. He made it back in the allotted time and Amos retied his hands. He didn't bother to do his feet because it would be hard to run through the willows bare-footed. Baldwin was released and given the same instructions.

When he got back Amos did not tie his hands, but handed him a cup of coffee and some hardtack. Baldwin practically inhaled it. Amos retied him and then fed Sanchez. He tied Sanchez again and sat them down near the fire.

"Now boys," Amos said over his coffee cup, "we have some things to work out. Do either one of you have a price on your head?" They both shook their head no. "That makes things a bit easier," Amos said and smiled slightly. "If you did, I would just shoot you and turn you in for the reward." He shrugged slightly. "You got any other horses hid away somewhere?"

"We have eight up by Lingle," Sanchez answered quickly. A quick frown from Baldwin showed that he had not wanted to reveal their treasure.

"So," Amos said and looked off into the sky as if he were thinking. "I could just shoot you, take your horses and gear, probably find those other horses and make some pretty good money." Sanchez's eyes were wide with fear and Baldwin clenched his jaw in anger. "There's only one thing to keep me from doing that," he said and paused long enough for what he was saying to sink in. "I want to get in with Middleton and his Pony Boys. Right now I figure I have more chance if I keep you alive." He looked at Baldwin; his jaw had relaxed slightly. "Him, I don't need," Amos said casually, drew his pistol and gestured toward Sanchez who was shaking so bad he could hardly stand up.

"Hi-yeee!" Sanchez wailed as he fell to his knees half sobbing and half praying. Amos cocked his pistol, but then stopped as if he were thinking it over. Baldwin's eyes were wide and he was shaking. Amos let enough time go by for the threat to have full effect. He let the hammer down on his pistol and looked at the two.

"I'll tell you what I'll do," he said, then paused as if thinking again. "You two agree to get me to Middleton or someone close to him and I'll let you live. I'll throw my two horses in with yours and any others we can pick up. We'll head for the Black Hills, and see what Middleton has to offer. We can split everything three ways. The more horses we have the more serious he'll take us." He paused again. "Before you agree, you think about this," Amos growled. "It wasn't too hard to get the jump on you two yesterday. If I had wanted you dead you would already be lying stiff on the ground and the buzzards would have ya. If you ever try to double cross me I'll kill the both of you without even thinkin' about it." He waited for his words to take effect. "Do we have a deal?" They both nodded rapidly.

CHAPTER 19

WHITE HORSES (1878)

mos started to cut them loose. "Boys, you have contacts and I have contacts," he said and smiled in a way that he hoped was menacing. "If we work together, I do believe we can make a lot of money." Their wrists were untied and they rubbed feeling back into their hands. "You boys sit yourselves down there for a minute and get your boots on." They did so as Amos walked over to the stream and retrieved their knives. "Here you go." He tossed their four knives between them. "Let's get saddled up and going," he said and grinned in the friendliest way he had for two days. "We've got money to make!"

In a few minutes they were saddled up and ready to go. "What about our guns?" Baldwin asked. Amos went over to the pile, untied them and handed them back to their owners. "Well what about some shells?" Baldwin sounded whiny. "These ain't much good without something to shoot in em."

"Couple of things about that, boys." Amos sounded bored. "Until I get real comfortable with you two, I'll just keep track of your ammunition until you need it. And, judging by the condition of your guns, neither one of you is much of a gun hand. Keep that in the back of your mind if you decide to alter our partnership." Amos motioned toward the hole in the dark man's hat.

Jose Sanchez had not wanted to say very much, but the two dark little eyes peering out from under his wide brimmed and now ventilated hat told Amos that Sanchez now ranked him just under the devil himself. The plan was beginning to unfold. "Soon," Amos thought to himself as they rode northward toward Lingle.

North of Hawk Springs, Horse Creek makes a large loop of about fifteen miles. By riding east across the loop to Dry Creek, they cut about ten miles off of their trip. A few miles downstream Dry Creek joined Horse Creek, and a few miles further downstream was the ranch were Sanchez and Baldwin had their horses. Just as Sanchez said, there were eight horses feeding in a fenced meadow. Most were young and of varying quality. Amos turned his two horses in with the rest.

"Not too bad," he said as he closed the gate. "I've seen better and I've seen worse." He paused and thought about it for a few seconds. "It ain't easy to divide ten horses between three people," he said as he got the sack he had put their ammunition in and laid it on the ground. Then he swung up into his saddle. "You two take care of the horses and round up some food." Amos tried to sound very authoritative. "I'll be back in the morning with a couple of horses so we can have a nice round number." He tapped Daniel on the flanks and was quickly gone.

He let his horse lope until they were out of sight and out of range, then slowed to a nice walk. "Daniel, old friend," Amos said as he took a deep breath and let it out, then slumped a little bit in the saddle. "I don't think I like being a horse thief." He rode northwestward until he came to the North Platte River then followed a wagon road upstream until he came to a ranch. There he offered to buy two horses, but was turned down. He rode on again until he came to a second ranch where he had better luck. The price was a little high, but Amos had no choice. However, to sweeten the deal, the owner of the ranch, a man named Lansky, put Amos up for the night, including supper and breakfast the next morning. Just after noon Amos had made it back to the stolen herd.

His two reluctant business partners were where he had left them. They opened the gate as Amos rode in at a trot, leading the two horses by makeshift halters. "That makes it a dozen!" Amos hollered as he looked back over his shoulder the way he had come. "I think we best be getting a move on, 'cause there might just be some unfriendly people behind me!" He started getting the pack horse ready to go. Baldwin and Sanchez were wide-eyed and slack-jawed. Amos glared at them and growled, "I told you to get ready to go, now move!"

"But Señor Mason," Sanchez's voice showed that he was truly afraid. "Look at the brands. Those are Lansky horses! If he catches us he will hang us for sure!"

"Sounds like an Irishman I know," Amos thought to himself as he smiled. "One name of Cullen." he glared at Sanchez and Baldwin. "He might catch you, and he might hang you," He said, his voice lowered in anger. "But if you don't get a move on, there won't be any might about it. You can be damned sure I will shoot you right here." His hand fell on his revolver and he flipped the safety strap off with his thumb. In ten minutes they were saddled and had the horses grouped up. By evening they had crossed the North Platte River and were on Sheep Creek.

They followed Sheep Creek north as far as they could, then when water started getting hard to find they pushed northwest to Red Cloud Creek. There was still water in the slough where the creek started. They had not been pushing hard, but they laid over an extra day before moving north to the Niobrara River near the settlement of Van Tassell. They skirted the town and then followed Van Tassel Creek north into the Hat Creek Buttes; after that they slowed down. When they eventually crossed over and got into Indian Creek they kept working north from one spring site to the next and finally came to Mule Creek, which they followed to its junction with the Cheyenne River. There they picked up the Cheyenne to Deadwood stage route and followed it north to the Stockade fork of Beaver Creek. They finally came to Canyon Springs Prairie. On the northwest end they found a canyon that was suitable to hold horses in. Several weeks had passed and their herd had grown to twenty seven animals. Each time Sanchez or Baldwin came in with a horse Amos would keep track of about where they were and what the brand was. Besides Lansky's horses, he had purchased five additional animals along the way just to keep up his part of the bargain. He was very much looking forward to having this part of his job over.

Baldwin said that he had a contact in Deadwood, so Sanchez was left to watch the horses while he and Amos rode to town. Amos had somewhat mixed feelings about going into Deadwood.

He certainly wanted to find Baldwin's contact and do what he could to help set up the apprehension of Middleton. On a more personal level he wasn't sure how bad he wanted to be in the town where Jim Hickok had been murdered. In any case, he needed to get a telegram to Nathan Tower and the rest of the lawmen in Laramie.

It was about thirty five miles to Deadwood from where the horses were, but it was all a wagon road and most of it was in good shape. Amos and Baldwin left early and made good time. They were in Deadwood in time for supper. Deadwood was a mining town, and was even wilder than Laramie had been when Amos first got there. There was almost nowhere to sleep, but there were more than enough saloons and brothels to take care of the miners. As it almost always was in the boomtowns where men hunted metal, the real money was to be made by relieving the miners of what they had worked so hard for, "Mining the miners", as it was known.

They sat in a tent café eating a meal that was twice as expensive as it should have been and half as good. Amos sat swirling his coffee, which was about all it was good for, and looking far away.

"You look like something's bothering you," Baldwin said to Amos. "You ought to be happy! We've just about got this over with."

"A friend of mine died here," Amos said and looked straight back at him. "I was just thinking of trying to find his grave. You know, to pay my respects and all."

"Well, when we get done here," Baldwin said and gestured toward his food, "I'm going to go get a bottle and then I'm going to find the cutest whore in this rat hole and try to be totally exhausted by tomorrow morning." He laughed. "Why don't you and me just meet back here about noon tomorrow. You can do what you want and I can do what I want," he said pleadingly to Amos. "Just for today." Amos acted reluctant, but was more than glad to let him go so he would have time to visit the telegraph office.

"I don't care what you do with your time," Amos tried to sound remote. "But, before you go running off, why don't you find your buddy and see if he wants the horses. That way, if I get bored I can head back and start the horses this way."

"Well okay!" Baldwin said happily. "It'll just take me a few minutes to find out where he is. You wait here for a few minutes and I'll be back."

"I'll go you one better," Amos said and chuckled slightly. "I'll be in that saloon right over there across the street and down. You come back there in ten minutes and I'll buy you a drink to get you started on the evening. After that I'm going to take a bottle and go find a place to just relax."

Good to his word Baldwin was back in the allotted time. Amos was sitting in a corner with his back to the wall as usual. He noticed Baldwin come through the door and poured him a drink from the bottle he had already bought. Baldwin sat down and threw his hands up in resignation. "I guess old Smith moved on over to Hill City just two days ago," he said and reached for the drink. "I guess we'll just have to go over there and find him." They sat together and finished the drink making small talk about the trip to Hill City. Baldwin helped himself to a second drink, downed it and rose to go. "By the way," he said with a grin, "did you know you're sitting where Wild Bill Hickok was when he got shot?" He chuckled, waved goodbye and went out the door. Amos felt a chill go up his spine and could not move away fast enough.

Amos figured that the chair incident was some sort of sign, so he inquired about the grave site and found that Jim Hickok had been buried in the Ingleside Cemetery upon his death. However a close friend, Charlie Utter, had recently moved the body to a plot at the newly constructed and much nicer Mount Mariah Cemetery. He inquired about directions and found that the cemetery was on the east side of town. His horse was still saddled and he rode out to find the plot. When he did, he stood at the foot of the grave for a long time thinking about where he had come from and all the things that had happened since he left Arkansas. It was quite likely that he owed his life to Jim Hickok. Finally he felt the chill of the night breeze and decided it was time to look for a place to sleep. "Well, old friend," he said to the grave as his eyes misted up, "I guess you have to let go of the past just to have a future. Rest well."

He went back in the trees not far from town and found a place to camp. That night before he fell asleep, he composed a message to send to Nathan Tower. The next morning he went immediately to the telegraph office and sent his message:

Sam Croft stop Laramie Wyoming stop I have twenty seven horses available including three white ones stop available near Hill City South Dakota stop please advise how many you want and at what price stop Amos Smith Mason stop.

He waited for some time until he got his return message. It read:

Amos S. Mason stop Deadwood South Dakota stop need twenty two but will probably take all including the white ones stop price forty dollars depending stop will be there first of the month stop please advise stop S. Croft stop.

Amos knew Sam had realized that Smith was in Hill City. A little later in the morning he found Baldwin, in a little worse condition, at the tent café. They poured down bad coffee and ate worse pancakes, then saddled up and headed back to Canyon Springs Prairie.

CHAPTER 20

THE WIND AGAIN (1878)

Baldwin was still hung over and not feeling quite right and Amos was in no hurry. It would be eight days before Sam Hanley would be there. They were obviously planning on traveling fast and light because they had given themselves so few days to be there, including the day that Amos had received the telegram. They would need to cover more than thirty miles a day on horseback. Amos knew the two men were very capable of doing it. Still, it did not leave much room for error.

They rode back the way they had come at an easy pace and were about halfway back when they decided to stop for the night. Camp was made by a small spring that had good water and Amos made coffee. He had bought a bag of biscuits and a small tin of preserves in Deadwood. These combined with some jerky and the coffee made supper. The same would be true for breakfast the next day.

Baldwin had been quiet most of the day, which Amos had taken as not feeling quite sober yet. However, as they were eating their supper Baldwin set his coffee cup down and looked at Amos. "I need to ask you about something," he said. He seemed very reluctant. "I happened to see you coming out of the telegraph office. Would you mind telling me why?"

Amos looked at him for a minute then reached in his shirt pocket and pulled out the return telegram and folded it out flat. That minute or so had bought him enough time to organize a story. "Sure," he said and handed the telegram over. Baldwin read it slowly. "When we first got together back there a few weeks ago, I told you I had contacts," Amos said. "That guy in the telegram is someone I've worked with before. I told him we have horses available and he told me how many he would take. Which is probably all of them and that surprises me. What's important is that he told me what he would pay for them. Now, when we talk to your man, we'll have two prices to compare so we can make the best money. It makes good business sense to me."

"Yeah," Baldwin said and handed the telegram back. "It makes good sense. I think you could've told me about it a little sooner."

Amos thought for a minute. "Yeah, I could have, maybe I should have," he said to Baldwin in a vaguely apologetic way. "I figured it was something I should share with you and Sanchez. Since you were a little on the 'exhausted' side today, I didn't want to overtax you by going through it now." Amos smiled at Baldwin and said, "I had intentions of telling you when we got back to the herd. I didn't see the sense in doing it twice."

Baldwin seemed happier. "What's that stuff about white horses?" he asked.

"Oh, that," Amos said as he smiled and chuckled. "He has this thing about white horses and even light-colored horses. He thinks they get snow blind easier and take more feed in the winter. It's something about them not being able to get as warm because of their color. Sounds like a bunch of crap to me. He's the one buying the horses and he can think anything he wants, as long as he has the money." Amos shrugged.

"Well, I never heard of such a thing," Baldwin muttered as he chuckled. "Why did he say he'd take them all anyway?"

"Two reasons," Amos said as he glanced at Baldwin. "He's trying to make it look like he's doing me a favor. And at the price he offered, he knows he can make a few bucks on any of those horses anyway."

"It did seem a might bit low to me," Baldwin said. "What are you going to tell him?"

"In the telegram," Amos said tapping on his shirt pocket, "it says to advise him. If I don't send a telegram back in a few days he'll know I sold them elsewhere." Amos glanced at Baldwin in a questioning way. "I don't suppose you know what your man is willing to pay?" he asked.

"No, I don't," Baldwin said and shrugged. "But even if it's a dollar more a head, that's still a good chunk of money. And now we have your telegram to help push the price up a little. I guess that was a pretty good move you made there, partner." Baldwin grinned. Amos hoped he had bought the story.

The next day they found Jose Sanchez taking care of the horses in the canyon. Over the evening meal everything that had happened was explained to him. The decision was made to spend a couple of days moving the horses close to Hill City. That way, regardless of who bought them, they could be delivered quickly.

Amos needed to stall for some time. He still had the bottle he had bought in Deadwood, and it was still almost full. He made a show of presenting it to Sanchez in payment for not getting to go to Deadwood. To his surprise, Baldwin had most of a fifth of whiskey in his saddle bag, which he brought out to help celebrate whatever it was they were celebrating. Amos slowly babied two drinks while the other two polished off the remainder. It was surprising that Baldwin was in the mood to drink again so quickly after his night at the brothels in Deadwood. Regardless of the reasons, neither one of them felt too much like pushing horses the next day, and Amos feigned a hangover to go along with them. He made coffee but nothing else, and they "recovered" most of the day; occasionally checking the horses, drinking water, sipping coffee and chewing on hardtack or jerky. The plan had worked and Amos had stalled for an extra day. Still, he was a day short.

Toward evening they were all feeling better and the plan was made to get the horses moving first thing in the morning. It was about thirty five miles to Hill City and, by taking three days they could move along easily. By moving slowly the horses would be in good shape to show a buyer. They did not get moving until midmorning, but quickly covered about twelve miles and made camp along Beaver Creek. The next day they made another twelve miles and camped along Castle Creek, and on the third day they camped along Newton Fork Creek just west of Hill City.

It was the morning of the eighth day and Amos wasn't sure if Hanley had made it to town. It did not seem likely that they would be there before evening. Amos did not hurry to have breakfast and poked fun at the suggestion that they go into town and have a decent meal. It was unlikely that there would be such a thing in the tiny mining camp, and even if there was it would undoubtedly be very high priced. They made do with bacon, beans and biscuits. Near midmorning Amos and Baldwin rode into town, again leaving Sanchez to tend the horses. Amos felt bad, in a way, about always leaving the stocky little Mexican with the herd, but he seemed to prefer staying out of sight as much as he could.

They rode into town, slow and easy, trying not to draw attention to themselves. They had a drink in the tent that served as a saloon, and sat listening until they figured out where Smith would be. To their chagrin he was in another tent saloon that was right across the street. They walked in to see a stocky man, with reddish brown hair and a beard to match, sitting at a makeshift table between two other men.

Amos had thought that Baldwin already knew Smith; instead he walked up and introduced himself just as any stranger would. Jim Baldwin mentioned his brothers, Johnny and Allen. Small talk was bandied back and forth for several minutes before the conversation turned to horses. The negotiations drug on until midafternoon. Amos said very little, but did produce the telegram showing the minimum price of the horses. A price of forty five dollars per horse and fifty dollars for the best ones was finally established. Arrangements were made for the horses to be inspected and picked up at midmorning the next day.

They found out that there actually was a decent place to eat and decided to have a meal before they headed back. They also decided to pick up what could easily be carried and take it back to Sanchez. The "restaurant" was actually three tents that had been erected in a T shape so that the doors all faced each other. The middle one was the cook tent and the others were dining halls. It was run by two heavyset women that spoke with what Amos thought was the same German accent that Barron Ignatz von Kramer of the Dead Buzzard Ranch had. Several children, who were apparently theirs, were doing dishes and tending tables. They were probably making more money than their husbands, who were miners. The food was pricey, but was good and very substantial. Amos got them to wrap up a good meal to take to Sanchez.

As they rode out of town they passed six men who were just riding in. Baldwin nodded and looked away. Amos basically ignored Sam Hanley, Bill Lykins, Riley and three other men he did not know. They rode quietly back to camp and gave the much welcomed meal to Sanchez. The day's events were reported, but very little else was said. There was something of a letdown because the operation was almost over.

Amos thought he would sleep well that night, but he didn't. Everything that had happened since he left Laramie kept playing over and over in his mind. He did not get to sleep until well after midnight and he awoke feeling tired. Sanchez had already made coffee, fried some bacon and made it into a sort of sandwich with some flatbread. Amos ate it and went to saddle his horse. He had just finished pulling up the cinch and had dropped the stirrup back down when something slammed across his back. He fell down, raised to his hands and knees, and then Baldwin kicked him in the stomach.

"You son of a bitch, you son of a bitch, you son of a bitch!" Baldwin screamed at him. "Do you think I don't know who that was?" Amos could not answer. "That's Sam Croft, the guy who used to run the WIND Ranch! You son of a bitch, you were going to work with him and cut us out of this!" Baldwin was still holding the rifle he had used to hit Amos with. "Well, you son of a bitch, this is going to work the other way!" Baldwin chambered a round into the rifle. "Me and Sanchez are gonna be splitting the money two ways, you son of a bitch!" He grinned at Sanchez.

"No, no!" Amos barely had air to speak. "Let me show you the paper." He started to reach into his shirt.

"What the hell paper are you talking about?" Baldwin pointed the rifle slightly away and stepped towards Amos.

"This one!" Amos barely whispered as he came up with his father's old Derringer. He swung up as hard as he could and broke the leather thong that held the gun around his neck. The uppercut caught Baldwin in the crotch just as Amos pulled the trigger. Baldwin's arms flew up and the rifle tumbled away. Amos stood up and brought an overhand right, Derringer and all, as hard as he could into Baldwin's left eye. As the barrel drove inward he pulled the trigger. The little rim fire pistol did not carry much power, but at that range just the concussion would be deadly and the bullet carried well into Baldwin's brain. Baldwin staggered backwards and Amos heard Sanchez cock his pistol. He fell to the ground just as the gun went off. The shot meant for Amos hit Baldwin square in the chest and knocked him over backwards. Sanchez was making the same "hiyee" sound he had made when Amos had threatened to shoot him. He fired again and the bullet went just over Amos's head. He began to cock his pistol again. Amos was just drawing his own pistol when he heard another much heavier shot. Sanchez spun around and fell to the ground. He grabbed his right shoulder with his left hand and lay there screaming as blood came through his fingers.

Amos had his pistols drawn and was still on the ground. He could see no one close by but then, over two hundred yards away, a man slowly stepped from behind a tree with his hands above his head.

"Don't shoot me brother!" he yelled. "I'm just here to buy a few horses." Riley cradled his Sharps and started towards Amos.

CHAPTER 21
THE WILL TO LIVE (1878)

"Riley, it's good to see you!" Amos extended his hand to Riley and then hugged him. It was like the weight of the world had been lifted from his shoulders. Sam Hanley came walking up with another man that he introduced as J.L. Smith.

J.L. Smith extended his hand. "It's really too bad we're going to have to arrest you," he said, shaking his head. "But that's what we have to do with horse thieves." He was trying not to laugh.

"Show me the horse you think I stole," Amos said with a smile. "And I'll show you the horse that I bought and have papers for."

"You bought horses?" Hanley asked. "Why?"

"Because, I'm not a horse thief!" Amos heavily emphasized "not". "Now then, do any of you guys know someone that needs nine horses?"

The three of them were laughing. "Sell them for what you can get out of them," Hanley said. "I'll make sure you get paid for the difference." Just then Sanchez groaned and they went to tend to him. They did what they could for him, but it was obvious that the Sharps Express round had nearly taken the arm off. At the very least, it would not be useful again. In fact, it would probably be lost. Amos felt bad about it because Jose Sanchez had been little more than a sidekick to Baldwin. Now he would go to prison and when he got out there would be little work he could do with just one arm.

When he brought it up Hanley shook his head and said, "I told Riley not to kill him, but that Sharps rifle has a lot of hit to it. You were almost in line with him. I couldn't take a chance on hitting you, and I didn't trust my Winchester at that range. There is a good chance that he has information that could get us closer to Middleton." He paused and looked at the unconscious Sanchez. "It isn't always pretty, Amos," he said. "Just remember that he chose the life he was living and that he might have killed you if Riley had not shot. Granted, death would probably have been kinder to him than this, but worse things have happened to a lot better men for a lot less reason."

Smith looked up from working on the wound and said, "Bill Lykins is in Hill City and has Smith. He's being guarded by him and the other deputized men. He wants to take him to the prison in Laramie. After the last fiasco in Nebraska, he doesn't really trust the Sheriff in Sidney. Besides, it isn't that much further to Laramie anyway. I think its best that we get as far away from here as we can, as quick as we can. Smith might just have some friends that are willing to try to help him."

"You did an excellent job Amos," Hanley said. "There's just one last part of this I'd like to have your help with. I'd like you to trail the horses back to their rightful owners. If you and Riley and a few of the other men would do that I would appreciate it. And I'll make sure you get paid well, on top of whatever rewards there are."

Amos looked at Riley, who nodded yes. Amos nodded to Hanley and said, "It will be nice to be riding with the law instead of running away from it." There was great relief in his voice.

In the time it took to pack up their camp and round up the horses, Lykins and the rest of the men had arrived from Hill City with their prisoner. Not only was Smith handcuffed and tied through the saddle's gullet, his feet were also manacled beneath the cinch. One of the men led the horse while another rode behind or beside him with a rope around the prisoner's neck. Lykins was not taking a chance on losing Smith again.

Sam Hanley volunteered to take Sanchez and the now deceased Baldwin to Rapid City, a distance of about twenty five miles. As a United States Federal Marshall he would be able to turn in the body and forward any reward money to Amos and the other men. He could get Sanchez some medical attention and question him when he was in better condition. He would end up behind Amos and the horses, but they would be traveling slowly and he would catch them in a few days. "I'd like to get back to Wyoming as quickly as possible," Hanley said. "I have not had the best of luck with law enforcement people in this part of the world. You guys get started back today and I will catch up to you somewhere over around Stockade Beaver Creek."

"It isn't going to make too much difference now," J.L. Smith said as he looked up and shrugged. "Sanchez just died. I think he had probably just lost too much blood."

"He probably lost the will to live too," Amos replied and looked away. "I guess death was kind after all," he said under his breath. There was a shovel on one of the pack horses. Amos got it and started digging a grave.

Lykins looked questioningly at him. "Why are you bothering?" he asked. "They were just horse thieves. We'll pile a few rocks over them and get going."

"You're right," Amos said looking very intently at Lykins. "They were just horse thieves and not the best of people, but they were people. They were someone's son and probably someone's brother. Maybe even a father. I doubt that their families will hurt any less because of the occupation that these two were in. I spent quite a bit of time with them and got to know them. That's more than I can say about you, and I would dig your grave if you fell over dead right now."

Lykins hung his head and turned away. Another shovel and a pick suddenly appeared. In two hours the outlaws had been buried. Amos made sure that Jose Sanchez's hat with the hole in it was buried with him. No one seemed to have any words to say, but each man, including Lykins took off his hat and stood silently by the fresh graves for a moment or two.

As Amos took off his hat to show his respect, he noticed a hole in it just at the peak of the crown. "I guess we're even, Jose," Amos said with a smile. Somehow he felt a little bit relieved.

There was still plenty of daylight to get headed back. Amos had saddled up the horses that he and the two horse thieves had been using and packed up the camp. Hanley came over to Amos and put his hand on his shoulder. "That was a fine thing you did burying those two," he said. "You sure took Billy Lykins down a notch or two and sometimes we all need that. It's too easy to get to thinking that the bad guys aren't human too. The only difference is in the choices we've made." He looked at Amos and nodded. "I'll fill out an affidavit stating that those two were killed and buried by you and these other men," he said. "If there is a reward it will come to you and you can do what you want with it."

"I'll just split it with everybody," Amos said sadly. "If I knew where Sanchez came from I might just send a share of it to his family." Amos was looking across the small valley where the horses grazed. "I don't think he ever knew anything. He was just trying to make a living. He only did what he was told to do. If I knew where he came from I would send a letter to his family telling them that he got killed in a horse accident."

The Marshall nodded to him. "I can probably find out where he came from for you," Hanley offered. "That's pretty big of you, considering he tried to shoot you."

Amos just shrugged and finished up with his horse. "He was scared to death, Sam," he said as he finished with his saddle. "He was shaking so bad, I don't think he could have hit anything, 'cept maybe my hat." Amos laughed. "I really wish we could have just caught him and sent him back to Mexico," Amos said and shrugged again. "That wasn't going to happen anyway. He would probably have spent quite a bit of time in prison. Hell, they might even have hung him. It probably worked out for the best just like it happened." Sam Hanley smiled and nodded.

It was after noon, but the days were still long and the horses knew where they were going. When they came to the area where they had spent the night on Castle Creek they naturally spread out and began to feed. It was a good enough place to spend the night. Smith was securely manacled and handcuffed to a large tree and two guards were kept on him. During the time the graves were being dug, two men had been sent to Hill City to get supplies. In addition, a deer had been shot near camp and it was being roasted in large pieces over a fire. Biscuits, beans, fried potatoes and onions and good coffee along with the deer made an excellent meal. Amos asked for a section of the ribs; it reminded him of his family at the White Rocks.

Amos realized how good it was to be among honest men again. He was soon drowsy and went to bed early and slept better than he had in a long time. When he finally woke up the next morning, breakfast was ready and his horses had been saddled for him. Riley came over with two cups of coffee. "We figured you needed some sleep," he said as he handed a cup to Amos. "It must have been tired sleep, because it obviously wasn't beauty sleep." He grinned and Amos laughed.

"You don't realize how tired you get always having to look over your shoulder," Amos said as he sipped his coffee. "I haven't felt this relaxed since I left Laramie."

"Well, we have more than enough people to push these horses along," Riley said. "Lykins says that once we get to Wyoming, he's going to take two or three men and get Smith to the prison." He paused, thinking. "Smith's not saying anything now, maybe he thinks he's going to be rescued or something. Once Lykins gets him to the prison, a little time in solitary confinement should get him talking."

The man who had been doing the cooking brought a large plate of food to Amos. It was much the same as they'd had the night before with a little bit of bacon thrown in. By the time Amos finished eating it was almost time to go. All he had to do was roll up his bedroll and tie it on the pack horse.

It was not far to Canyon Springs Prairie and there was no need to hide the horses, so they camped near the head of Stockade Beaver Creek. Amos was about to unsaddle his horse when Sam Hanley came over to him. "Before you do that, could you take me to where you were hiding the horses?" he asked. "There's a good chance I might be up this way again and I'd like to know the lay of the land." They got Riley and rode the short distance east to the canyon. Hanley looked it over closely and inspected the routes in and out. "I can see why you chose it," he said as he looked around. "It's got good feed, good water and it's hard to see if you're not right on top of it."

"Maybe we should call it Horse Thief Canyon," Riley said with a laugh. "That sounds better than Thieving Amos Gully." They all laughed, got some fresh spring water in their canteens, and rode back to their camp.

That evening as they ate supper Hanley came over and sat next to Amos. "Here," he said and handed two pieces of paper, one with something wrapped in it, to Amos. "These will help keep you out of trouble, I hope." The first paper was written on official letterhead and explained that Amos was acting on behalf of the U.S. Marshall in returning the horses that had been stolen. The second was a list of the ranches that the brands on the horses indicated, as well as where they were located.

The object was a Deputy U.S. Marshall's badge. Amos folded the two pieces of paper and put them in his pocket. "I'm sorry Sam," he said as he handed the badge back to Hanley. "I appreciate the offer, but I'm not meant to be an officer. I have trouble enough doing the work I do without that on top of it."

"I'm not asking you to be a permanent deputy," Sam said, but did not take the badge back. "It's just until you get back to Laramie. It will make you look a lot more official when you take the stolen horses back. It might keep you from getting shot. That's what I meant by keeping you out of trouble." Amos slipped the badge into his pocket.

The next morning Bill Lykins, Sam Hanley and J.L. Smith rose early and started toward Laramie with Smith. Again, the prisoner was handcuffed, manacled and securely tied to his saddle. The man behind Smith again placed a rope around his neck and carried a rifle over his saddle pointed at him. Even if a rescue attempt came, it was unlikely that Smith would survive it.

As much as Amos liked Sam Hanley, he was glad to see them go. The only thing he envied was that they would be back in Laramie in just a few days. Meanwhile, Amos would take a couple of weeks to return the stolen horses to their rightful owners, and get his little unwanted herd home. The Black Hills were however beautiful and it was a good day to be on a saddle horse.

CHAPTER 22

PUPPIES (1878)

Counting the horses that had been stolen, and the ones Amos had bought, plus the horses the outlaws had owned that had been given to Amos, they were now herding thirty horses. And that did not count the horses and pack horses the deputies had or those that originally belonged to Amos and Riley. Amos has been in the lead while the horses were being trailed back to the head of Stockade Beaver Creek. After that it was entirely obvious which way they should go, so it didn't matter very much who was in the lead. Amos took his turn riding flank and drag along with everyone else. They made about twenty five miles down the creek and came to a bend that made a natural place to hold the horses. According to the list, one of the ranches from which horses had been stolen was only a couple of miles away. Amos left the rest of the men to tend the horses and make camp while he rode on to talk to the owners.

He explained the situation to the ranch owners as best he could, but they were naturally suspicious until he showed them the papers. He had nearly forgotten about the badge, so when he reached in to put the papers back in his pocket he pinned it in place. He held back his jacket to show the badge and that seemed to ease the situation. The ranch owners were invited out to look at the horses and take back what belonged to them. Amos also let them know that there were several other horses that would be for sale. That evening they rode out and took back three horses, two of which were their own and one that belonged to Amos. "That's one down, and too damn many to go," he thought to himself as he watched the ranchers ride away.

By the time they got to the North Platte River they were down to eight of the stolen horses and twelve that were legitimate. They had followed the route Amos and the horse thieves had taken in reverse except that they had not come down Sheep Creek but had gotten into Rawhide Creek and followed it to the North Platte River. When they crossed the river they were very close to the ranch where Amos had bought his first two "stolen" horses. He decided to go and talk to the rancher named Lansky, whom Jose Sanchez had been so afraid of. The old cowboy had seemed like a good enough man when Amos bought horses from him.

Amos rode into the ranch yard and dismounted. Two men covered him with shotguns, but when the old man came out he waved them away. "Amos, I didn't think I would ever see you again," Lansky said as he motioned him to the porch. "Come on up here and sit down." Amos was surprised that he had been re-membered, and did as he was told. Soon someone brought them each a glass of cool water. Amos showed Lansky the papers and his badge and explained the situation. "I knew something wasn't quite right that night you came in here," Lansky chuckled. "But I wasn't going to turn down good money like that for those two horses. Now, what is it that you want me to do?"

"Well Sir," Amos began. "I still have those two horses and they served me well. I also have a number of other horses and some tack that I would like to sell off. I'm not trying to push anything on you, but if you have need for a few horses I'm sure I could make you a deal that would be hard to pass up."

"Hell of a horse thief you are!" The old man laughed and hol-lered at one of his men to saddle up a horse. In a few minutes they were on the way back to the camp. It was pretty easy to see that the old rancher had spent a lot of time in a saddle. Lansky took his time looking at the horses and about one minute each for the saddles. "Well, old son," he said. The title reminded Amos of Patches Johanson. "Some of them are good, some of them are just horses. I'll tell you what, I'll give you forty five dollars apiece straight across for everything and that much for each of the saddles, with the bridles and everything. That might be a little cheap, but you won't have to fool with them anymore." Amos looked questioningly at him. Lansky caught it. "Okay," he said. "I'll sweeten the pot just a little." The old rancher was a businessman. "I noticed that there are eight other horses in there with brands from ranches around here. I figure those are the stolen horses, and they are the bunch you are planning to take back. I get along pretty good with those ranchers and I'll take their horses back for you. You boys run them in tomorrow morning along with everything else, and you can pack up and head for home. I'll even stake the bunch of you to breakfast before you go."

It sounded too good to be true to Amos, but he stood around for a minute as if he were thinking about. "You've got a deal Sir," Amos said and extended his hand. That was all it took to make a deal with a man like Lansky.

The old rancher swung easily into his saddle. "Yep, Amos, you are one hell of a horse thief!" he said and laughed, spun his horse, touched spurs to his flanks and galloped off.

For the second time since Hill City a great weight had been lifted from Amos's shoulders. The other men had the horses settled and supper was going over the campfire. The sun was just setting and Laramie Peak was outlined on the horizon. Once the horses were delivered the next morning there would be no reason for the group to stay together. Everyone was talking about getting home as they sat eating supper around the fire. The more Amos looked at Laramie Peak the more he decided that would be a good way to go home.

They didn't need to be up real early the next morning, but everyone was excited and all of the horses were ready to go just as the sun lit the top of Laramie Peak. It seemed like another good sign to Amos. Apparently the hands at the Lansky Ranch got up pretty early too, because there was a corral open and a man holding the gate as Amos and his bunch came into the yard. The promised breakfast was basic; bacon, eggs, pancakes and coffee. It was good and there was plenty of it.

When they were finished Lansky thanked each of them. As they headed out the door he took Amos aside. "I don't generally pay in cash" he said and looked at Amos. "I usually have a draft against Tim Cullen's Bank in Laramie; but I figure you need to pay those boys and this will make it easier. If you come by here again be sure to stop. Now, you guys get on out of here, and have a safe trip home." He smiled and extended his hand to Amos.

Amos paid the men and watched as they rode off. He swung into his saddle and he and Riley headed up the North Platte River. "Riley, it feels so damn good not to be herding anything," he said and grinned widely. "Not to mention not having to look over my shoulder all the time. I don't think I'm going to want to play horse thief again for a long time." Riley laughed. The traveling was smooth so they set their horses on an easy lope and headed west towards Laramie Peak. They camped that night on Cottonwood Creek. The next day they made it easily to the LP Ranch.

Ned Hogan was his usual cautious self and met them with his shotgun in hand. As soon as he recognized his two friends, the shotgun was leaned against the cabin and he was down the steps to shake their hands as quickly as they dismounted. It was much cooler near Laramie Peak than it had been on the plains and coffee was the order of the day. This suited Amos fine because Hilda Hogan made some of the best coffee he had ever experienced; not a drop would ever go to waste from his cup.

Riley and Amos put their gear in the bunkhouse and took the opportunity to get cleaned up. Just as the sun set Burke and Barry Hogan rode in. It was just mid-September, but even so there was a touch of fresh snow on the very top of Laramie Peak. They had decided it would be a good time to get some supplies to Jacque LaRamie and his son Standing Bull. There were three different languages involved, but between them they had come up with enough of a communication system to get basic ideas across. Amos very much wanted to get Jacob together with them so the stories of what had happened over so many years could be preserved.

Mother Hogan, as Hilda was known, would not hear of Amos and Riley going to bed without supper. Neither one of the men was going to argue since they had eaten at the Hogans' before. They ate supper and were well into desert and coffee when a whining sound came from the kitchen. "Oh, that is that silly puppy dog again," Mother Hogan said as she got up and went to the kitchen.

Amos looked questioningly at Ned Hogan. "We found an old mother dog along the road to Cheyenne," he said. "She has four pups, but she can barely take care of two of them. I'm afraid we are probably going to have to get rid of the two littlest ones so the other two will have a chance. Even so, we'll have to give them milk. They're barely old enough to have their eyes open. I hate to do it, but I see no other way."

Riley looked at Amos. "Are you thinking what I'm thinking?" he asked and got up to head for the kitchen. On the floor near the stove on a pile of blankets, was a black-and-white dog with four puppies nuzzling at her breasts.

"Those are sheepdogs," Riley said as he gently touched each of them. The mother dog licked his hand. "Mac?" He looked up at Amos. Amos just smiled and nodded. The next morning they were on their way to Rock River. Mother Hogan had made a cloth cradle that would fit around the neck and shoulder of each of the men so he could carry a puppy inside his coat. She had also given them more than enough milk for two days. That night they camped at the same bend in the Laramie River where they had before. They took special care to make sure the puppies were warm and well fed. The next day they rode into Mac MacTavish's yard. Mac was standing at his forge with the doors to his shop swung open. When he saw them he came out with his arms spread to do his usual hug. They both backed away and held up a hand.

The big man's eyes widened as he looked at them. "Lads," he said with surprise. "Aire ye injured or just mad at me?"

"Not exactly," Amos said as they both opened their coats and rolled back the blankets to reveal the puppies.

"What have ye got there?" Mac said as he stepped forward to look. His eyes widened. "Why...why, those aire sheepdogs!" he exclaimed and reached to touch one. "Why," he cried as his eyes widened further, "those aire border collies! Oh, I have nay seen one of these since I left the old country! They're Scottish sheep-dogs ye know? Whatever aire ye going to do with them?"

"I was just going to ask you the same thing," Amos said. He could not help but grin as he held the puppy out to Mac.

Mac took a quick breath. "Ye don't mean…I…I mean…for us?" he said with his mouth open and a grin that went from ear to ear. He took a few steps towards the house and bellowed, "Missus, come quickly, bring the children!" In a moment they were out. Riley handed the little bundle to Mac's wife and Amos handed the other one to Mac.

"Oh-oh-oh," Was all she could say. She had her hand over her mouth as tears welled up in her eyes. She cradled the puppy and held it to her. The little dog licked her on the chin.

Mac handed her the second puppy; it was hardly bigger than his hand. She held them both to her much as Amos thought she must have held their twin boys when they were babies. "Look children," she said softly. "We have two new wee little sisters to care for."

CHAPTER 23

PLAID (1879)

"Well, that felt pretty good," Riley said as they rode along to Medicine Bow. "I never thought that a couple of little puppies could make so many people so happy."

"Yeah, they couldn't go to a better home," Amos said as he smiled on the outside and on the inside. "I think those two little puppies won the grand drawing." He thought about the evening before. They had eaten supper and were watching the children play with the puppies. Missus MacTavish sat in her beautiful rocker watching. When Amos and Riley stepped up beside her to watch she reached out and took their hands and held them to her. Amos knew by the small trembling he felt that she was saying thank you, but the words just wouldn't come out.

The next morning, when they came out from breakfast to saddle up, their horses were ready to go. Amos could see that there were new shoes on all three. He had started to thank Mac, but the big blacksmith shook his head and put his arms around both of them. Amos was beginning to lose his breath when Mac let go. "Now, ye will be stopping back by here soon," he said and grinned but there were tear tracks in the dust on his face. "Those two wee little ones will be growing quickly, and it will surprise ye how much they can learn."

"Are you sure those dogs are from Scotland, Mac?" Riley asked in a very serious voice.

"Of course I'm sure laddie," Mac said, somewhat affronted. "I was around many of them in the old country. Why would ye be asking?"

"Well, they're not wearing a dress," Riley said and broke into a grin. "And they're not plaid." He was now laughing.

Mac picked Riley up and set him on his horse. "Ye daft Irishman, tis not a dress, tis a kilt!" he said as a grin crossed his face. "And everyone knows they will nay turn plaid until they lose their puppy fur!" He slapped Riley's horse on the rump and laughed as he galloped away.

Amos got the rope for the pack horse, grinned at his big friend, and trotted off to catch Riley. They rode away with saddlebags that were much fuller than they had been, and the aroma was wonderful.

Ted Brow was at his usual place in the TIC Ranch office. He glanced up from the part of his job that he loathed, paperwork, and looked over his glasses at Amos and Riley. "Well Riley, he said, "I see you caught that damn horse thief. Scruffy looking character isn't he?" Amos realized he hadn't shaved or cut his hair since he'd left. Brow didn't crack a smile for a few seconds; then he started laughing. "Come on over here and let me shake your hand," he said. "I'd get up, but this damn leg is giving me hell today." Amos stepped up and reached across the desk to shake hands. "So tell me about it," Brow said, as he leaned back and put his hands behind his head.

It took a while, but Amos related the story of what had gone on during the summer. Then Riley told him about going to Hill City and the capture of Smith. Brow, of course, knew that the capture of Smith was the key to getting enough information to find Middleton. "I know they've got Smith at the prison," Brow said, still leaning back in his chair with his leg stretched out. "Sam Hanley will pretty much go by the book when it comes to questioning him, but I'd sure hate to be in Smith's shoes if Billy Lykins or Bill Llewellyn get ahold of him. One way or another, I imagine they're going to have all the information they can get by about the first of the year."

"So you don't think there'll be much going on before spring?" Amos asked.

"Well, I doubt it," Brow replied. "They're probably going to throw Smith in solitary confinement for a while and then work on him for a few weeks or even months. They can let Middleton settle down for a while. He's probably pretty shook up and on the watch right now. Regardless of what happens I can always call you two up and let you know if they need you." The idea of being "called up" was still very new and strange to Amos. The new telephone thing was going to take a lot of getting used to. Brow paused for a moment. "I'm afraid I have some bad news to give you," he said with a frown. "You remember that before you left Nathan Tower and Sam Hanley were working on a train robbery attempt that happened just east of here?" Riley and Amos nodded. Brow hung his head slightly and grimaced. "Well, Bob Widdowfield and Tip Vincent got killed trying to catch the men that did it. They got ambushed over in Rattlesnake Canyon."

Amos could hardly believe what he heard. He did not really know Tip Vincent well, but he had spoken to Deputy Bob Widdowfield many times and knew both to be good and dedicated lawmen. "They know who did it?" he asked.

"There was a gang of them," Ted Brow said to Amos. "The leader is Big Nose George Parrott. And his sidekick, Dutch Charley Burris, was in on it too. They got away and probably headed north. There's not much we can do about it now." He let a moment go by. "On a lighter note, I know it might be beneath the dignity of you two high-powered horse thief hunters, but Clancy could use a little help with the fall roundup. That is if you remember how to do it." He chuckled. "It might be good for you two just to go be cowboys for a while."

They went out to the dining area and bummed a cup of coffee from the cook and ate part of the "wee small snack" Missus MacTavish had sent with them.

"You know, Riley," Amos said as he felt something become empty inside him. "I've been in Rattlesnake Canyon dozens of times. If I had been here I might have been able to keep those two from getting killed."

"Amos," Riley said as he looked straight into the eyes of his friend. "I know that canyon at least as well as you do. I was here and nobody told me anything about it, so how could any part of this be your fault? You already stuck your neck a long ways out to get Smith. You just can't be everywhere at once and you can't take care of everyone the way you seem to think you should. Besides, they might have killed you too."

Amos shrugged. "Thanks Riley," he said as they went outside to get their horses. It was mid-afternoon when they started riding towards Carbon.

Breakfast had been huge and they probably hadn't really needed lunch. They were in no hurry and rode along slowly until their meal settled and then kicked into a fast walk. The crew of the Carbon Ranch had just come in, unsaddled and was in the dining hall about to eat when Riley and Amos walked in. Everyone was glad to see Amos back and healthy. Of course, he caught all kinds of grief about the long hair and beard. It was decided that he would have the next day off to get cleaned up and repair his equipment and clean up his guns. Old Charlie the cook took the opportunity to give them a bad time about making him set extra places. Amos had not realized how much he had missed being at the ranch and with his friends.

Amos wanted to talk with Jacob to see how the Children of the Mountain were doing. He was going to ask for enough time to ride to the upper ranch house. "There's no need to ride clear up there," Clancy said. "Just give me a minute, then come on into the office and you can talk to him." In about four minutes Clancy hollered for him to come in. He had Amos sit down in a chair near the telephone. "You talk into this," he said and pointed to the mouthpiece. "And you listen here." He put the earpiece in Amos's hand and held it up to his ear. "And don't yell, just talk clear."

It was hard to believe that he could hear Jacob on the other end. He found out that the Indians had not yet returned to the White Rocks, although Jacob had run into them further up the mountain and they were doing fine. He made arrangements to see Jacob when the roundup started to wind down. Amos had mixed feelings about the telephone. On one side he could see how much faster it made everything, but he also felt that something personal was lost by not being able to see the person he was talking to.

The roundup went well, mostly because the weather stayed good until the last week or so. Then a light snowstorm made it somewhat colder but not abnormally so. There had been a bumper crop of cattle that year and it took several days to get them all loaded on the trains at the Medicine Bow stockyard. When the last of the cattle were shipped, Ted Brow invited everyone to a large supper at the TIC Ranch office. He did however, stipulate that everyone needed to get thoroughly cleaned up, since few of them had taken time to do so since the roundup had begun.

There was only one bathtub available at the ranch house and only one available at the barbershop/bathhouse near the hotel. Cards were drawn to see who used the tub at the TIC house and the one in town. Amos was lucky enough to draw a position at the one in town and he took the opportunity to get a haircut and shave along with his bath. He was surprised at how much lighter he felt when he came out. Of course Riley had to pretend not to know him, even accusing him of being some saddle tramp trying to steal Amos's horse.

It was going to take way too long for everyone to get cleaned up, so the unlucky men went to the water tank for the train and jumped in, clothes and all. It was comical, since the water was about forty five degrees, and "refreshing" to say the least. In fact it probably got their clothes cleaner than they had been in weeks.

The meal was beef, cooked in about any way imaginable, with numerous side dishes and desserts. There was almost anything that could be thought of to drink, from water to rotgut whiskey. The year had been good and the TIC Ranch was showing its appreciation. When they finished eating, Ted Brow made a show of returning Amos's dark cavalry style hat to him. "It'll fit you now," he said with a laugh and pointed to Amos's freshly barbered hair. Everyone had a good laugh, including Amos.

Jacob was there, and he and Amos and Riley spent a long time going over everything that had happened. The stories of the summer were told, and many possibilities for what might come of it were pondered. Jacob thought that the Children of the Mountain would have probably returned to the White Rocks with the snow that had just fallen. They made arrangements to go and see them in the coming week.

The men from the Upper River Ranch, including Jacob had the furthest to go and left before eight o'clock in the morning. The men from the Carbon Ranch had only a few hours to ride and most of them, including Amos and Riley, hung around to have lunch on the left overs. Just past noon they saddled their horses for the ride back. Ted Brow limped onto the porch and hollered at them, "Tim Cullen is going to be here for the two weeks before the New Year. He sent word that he would like to talk to the three of you one day during that time. It probably won't take more than a few hours, but I think you need to plan for it now." They nodded and rode away.

Fall turned into winter and an invitation had come to attend Christmas dinner and the christening of the new child at the Tower residence. Jacob rode down from the Upper River Ranch and the three of them caught the train to Rock River. Amos had debated not stopping, but he wanted to see how the puppies had done. They walked the short distance to the MacTavish home. As they walked into the yard, two partially grown dogs bounded out towards them. Mac stepped out the front door and hollered, "Amos, Riley, sit down right there!" Amos looked at his friend with great surprise, but then the two puppies sat down.

"You named them Amos and Riley?" Riley sounded amazed. "Why would you do a mean thing like that?"

"How better to name them, than after the two men who probably saved their lives?" Mac asked with a smile. "Besides, tis the only way I can get any work out of someone by that name." He started laughing. "Come along now," he said and the two dogs got up and headed toward him. The big Scotsman laughed, "Ye see what I mean? Ye three might as well come too, Missus will be glad to see the lot of ye."

They went in the house. It was warm and smelled wonderful. Missus came out of her kitchen wiping her hands on her apron. "Ah, my boys are home," she said and smiled beautifully, her green eyes shining as she hugged each one of them. "Tis nay better Christmas present that I could have asked for." Her children were on the floor playing some sort of game. They took turns caring for the baby and the puppies sat next to them as if they were being guard dogs. Amos could not think of a better place to be.

They finished eating, way too much as usual, and went into the sitting room to talk to Mac. "Lads, we have been invited to the christening of the wee baby boy that Nathan Tower and his Missus have just had," he said. "I am sad to say that we will nay be able to be there. Ye see, several members of our families are going to be here and my Missus wants to show them a good Christmas." He shrugged his shoulders. "If I could prevail upon ye, I would like ye to deliver this for me." He got a box from a cabinet and handed it to them.

Jacob removed the top; inside was a plaid blanket. "Oh Mac," Jacob said as his eyes widened. "This is a Scottish infant blanket, and that plaid is the Tartan of your clan!"

"Aye, that it is," Mac said. He was obviously glad that Jacob had recognized what the gift was. "And tis the hunting tartan. In the old country the hunting tartan is given to male children to start them towards a manly way of life."

"But how did you know it was a boy?" Riley asked. "We haven't heard a word about it."

"There ye go being Irish again," Mac said feigning exasperation. "Obviously, my Missus told me." Riley gave him a questioning look. Mac rolled his eyes and said, "Ye poor daft lad. Someday ye will have a wife of your own, God help her, and ye will find out that they just know these things. Don't question it, just accept it, tis the way things aire." He laughed.

"If I'm not mistaken," Jacob said as he flashed a knowing smile. "Traditionally, by giving this blanket, you are saying that the child is a part of your clan. I do believe you have volunteered yourself and your clan to watch over Nathan's children no matter what."

The big man's eyes were watery. "Aye," he said solemnly. "That I have."

CHAPTER 24

THE ARTIST (1879)

After a very substantial breakfast, Mac gave them a ride into town to catch the train. By noon they were in Laramie and had secured rooms at the hotel. As usual the wind was blowing, and the western skies promised snow later in the day. They stopped by the Tower residence just long enough to say hello to Mary Beth and to see the new baby. Jacob gave her the gift from Mac and explained its significance. It was just a couple of days before Christmas, and the three of them did a little bit of last-minute shopping. A bottle of good whiskey was always a sure bet for Tom Sherman Senior at the livery stable as well as Sam Hawken the gunsmith.

Riley found an artist pad and some high-quality artist pencils at the general store. He bought them, had them nicely wrapped and took them to the livery stable for Olaf Nordquist. "After all the jokes we've made about him, and all the help he's been, this is the very least we can do." Riley said. He had planned to leave the gift anonymously at the livery stable, but just as he was leaving Olaf came in. "We just want you to know how much we appreciate everything you did for us," Riley said as he handed the package to Olaf. "Especially with old Patches."

Olaf unwrapped it right there. "Oh-oh my goodness!" he said as his face lit up at the sight of the drawing materials. "I never tot I vould have someting dis nice to draw vit. Dis is so nice, how can

I ever tank you? I haf noting to give you in return," he said mournfully. "Dat makes me feel so sad."

"I have an idea," Jacob said. "Do you think you could draw a couple of nice pictures of the three of us? We would like to have them framed and give them to Nathan and Mac."

"Oh yah, I can do dat in yust a few minutes," Olaf said. He was very happy to have someone interested in his work. "You tree yust stand out here in duh light and I vill be done in no time." He got them standing just as he wanted them and began drawing. True to his word, in less than fifteen minutes he had completed most of the first drawing. Then he had them change positions and quickly roughed out a second sketch. "Now den you can yust go along and I vill finish it up and make anoder vun," He said. "I vill find you later, at duh restaurant I tink, and give dem to you." He went back to his new drawing pad.

Jacob, Riley and Amos continued to walk around town looking at all the sights. They stopped by the gunsmith shop and gave Sam Hawken his present. He was grateful and reached under the showcase to bring up three boxes of 44.40 cartridges. He opened one of the boxes and took out a round. He held it up in the light so they could see it well. "Now, take a close look at the bullet," he said looking over his glasses. "You'll notice that the tip has been hollowed out; that's why they call them hollow points. They're lighter, faster and they expand very quickly. If you ever need to blow a very big hole in something or someone, this is the bullet that will do it. I heard about your run in with the Middleton bunch and what they did to old Patches Johanson." He looked over his glasses again. "I can't think of anyone I would rather give these to." They thanked him and went back out into the gathering gloom of evening. It was only five o'clock but the sun had long since set and the cold of the night was beginning to settle in. They headed for the restaurant.

They were half a block from the door when Olaf Nordquist ran up. He had the pictures completed and already framed. Amos had expected two pictures that would be just alike. What they got was the picture he had expected of the three of them leaning against the wall of the livery and, much to his amazement, the second was a picture of the three of them on their horses with the Medicine Bow Mountains in the background. Every detail was perfect. Olaf stood holding his hat in his hands, searching their faces for a sign of acceptance.

"I –uh," Jacob said looking at the picture with the horses. "I believe you are a genius when it comes to artwork."

"Does dat mean you like dem?" Olaf asked still searching their faces for approval.

"What it means," Riley said as he put his arm around Olaf's shoulder, "is that you have too much talent to be working in a livery stable. These are great!"

Amos walked up to Olaf. "Hold your hand out Olaf," he said. The artist did so and Amos laid a ten dollar gold piece in his palm. Olaf started to speak, but Amos quickly interrupted him. "If you try to say no I'm going to punch you right in the nose." He tried to look ferocious, but soon started chuckling.

Olaf's eyes got big, but after a minute a smile lit his face. "Tank you Mister Amos, tank you so very much," he said with tears in his eyes. "Now my little family vill have a vonderful Christmas."

Amos smiled, nodded and turned to walk away. In a few steps Jacob and Riley had caught up to him. Jacob caught them both by the shoulder and stopped, "My brothers," he said and smiled widely at both of them. "What you did back there was very kind. And yes, Riley, I saw you drop a gold piece in his pocket."

"Yeah, well," Riley said and grinned back at Jacob. "You're going to have to get a lot better at it than that if you're going to put one over on me. I saw you put one in his other pocket!" The three of them were laughing as they went into the restaurant.

They had not planned to eat very much in light of the meal they'd had with the MacTavishs, and the meal that was probably going to be served on Christmas Day. They ate small portions and had decided to pass on dessert. However, Elbert Richards the restaurant owner came in as they were finishing up their last cup of coffee and set a fruit cake on the table. It was full of fruits and nuts and all kinds of sweet things that they could not possibly leave alone. Elbert laughed and poured them another cup of coffee. By the time they left Amos was again far too full. "I must look like a waddling duck," he thought to himself, though not for the first time, as they walked back to the hotel. "My horse is going to hate me."

Christmas dinner was indeed wonderful and that evening they christened the new little boy. His name would be Mason Nathan Tower. His father liked the name that Amos had used as an alias. "Besides that," Nathan said as got into his monotone voice again, "someday I'm going to have to tell him the stories about you and me and that bunch of renegades you ride around with. This way he'll have a tie to it without feeling like he's been named after anybody." Amos just smiled and nodded.

That evening there were gifts for the children. Jacob went to Mary Beth where she was sitting in her rocking chair with both of her children. Her daughter slept in the beaver blanket that Jacob had brought her, and the new son lay in the Tartan blanket that Mac had sent them. From his pocket Jacob took two small soft leather pouches that had been beaded. "These are memory pouches," he said as he handed them to her. "This one, with the tiny shield, is for a boy so that he will be protected as he grows up. This one, with a circle on it, is for a girl because it represents the circle of life that only a woman can fulfill." He opened one and dropped two small beads in her hand. One was blue and the other pink. Each had a little bit of fine hair that had been sealed in. "These little hairs are from each of your children. There is an identical set in each pouch. I took the liberty of making these because I know that someday the brother and sister will look on them as a good memory."

"And just so you won't forget us," Riley walked over to her, grinning widely as he handed her the picture of the three of them leaning against the livery stable. "We had Olaf Nordquist draw this for you."

"Just what I needed," Nathan said flatly. "Another wanted poster." Everybody in the room was laughing. Nathan quickly found a place among the pictures of his family and hung it up.

The sun had long since set and it was time to leave Nathan and Mary Beth to themselves. They put on their jackets and were on the porch when Nathan stepped out. "Two things," he said. "First, I want to thank you. Nobody ever thinks up better gifts than you and Mac do. Those things will mean a lot forever. And second, I'm not going to talk business today, but Mister Cullen will be in town day after tomorrow and he wired me to let you know that he wants to talk to you."

"Not to talk business either, there, Sherriff," Riley said grinning and looking cross eyed, "I just wanted to let you know, we all voted for you again."

Nathan looked at Riley as if he were crazy. "There wasn't an election this year Riley." There was incredulousness in his voice.

"No wonder you won." Riley said. He looked at Nathan as if to say "gotcha" and started laughing. "It only took three votes to elect you." They were laughing as they shook hands and Amos and his brothers headed back to the hotel.

Amos slept well that night and dreamed of ravens, horses and black and white puppies. The next morning he sat having coffee with Jacob as they waited for Riley. "Jacob," Amos said. "That was a darn nice gift you got those kids. I'm just curious about how you got that little bit of hair from that tiny little baby."

Jacob smiled one of his "I'm going to teach you something" smiles. From his pocket he took a very small flake of stone wrapped in a small patch of leather. "This is extremely sharp and, the way it is shaped, it will stick on your finger with just a little bit of pitch. It was nothing to touch the children's faces and end up with a little bit of their hair," he said. He thought for moment. "You will remember a similar thing happening at Fort Steele some time ago, when two Indians escaped." He chuckled.

Two days later Cullen arrived on the morning train. He wasted no time in getting to his office at the bank and summoning Amos, Riley and Jacob. "Sit down gentlemen," he said, smiling as he motioned them to three chairs in front of his desk. "Let me start off by saying that the way you analyzed the situation for my good friend Ned Hogan and the way you worked it out, was far, far, better than I had hoped for. He has told me how grateful he is and I am passing that on to you." He became more serious. "Now then, even though he eventually escaped, I'm still quite happy with your role in the capture of Doc Middleton and some of his men. The same can be said about the recent recapture of Smith and the other horse thieves. I received a telegram expressing the gratitude of old Lansky and several of the other ranchers." He paused.

"On a slightly darker note, as I understand it Will Llewellyn and Billy Lykins have been having, shall we say, vigorous discussions with Mister Smith at the prison. I understand also that quite a bit of information has been forthcoming. They are looking for a little bit more information on Middleton's exact location, but it appears that another expedition will be mounted against Middleton and his group sometime this coming summer. Billy Lykins and, of course, Sam Hanley were quite impressed with you and Riley in Nebraska and would like you to join them again this summer. The final decision is again yours, but as for me, I would encourage you to go. Doc Middleton and his men have been more than just an aggravation to me." He stopped for a minute to gather his thoughts. "Jacob, I will assume that your position on this is unchanged, and that is completely acceptable to me," he said to Jacob, who nodded. "Sam Hanley will notify you when the time comes. There is significant reward money offered for Middleton and some of his gang. I don't know how that money will be divided up, so, I will match any money that is awarded to you three. Of course, your word as to the actual events will be good enough for me." The three men nodded.

"Now then, onto something cheerful," he said as he gathered a handful of papers from his desk and gave them each a part of it. "These are summations of your financial standings within this bank and the other holdings I have invested in for you. Without going into a lot of detail, which I'm sure Jacob could do for you, I will simply say that you are all doing quite well."

It might as well have been written in Chinese for Amos, and Riley was doing little better. Jacob, of course, was going through it page by page and quickly too. In just a few minutes he had finished. "Thank you Mister Cullen," Jacob said as he looked up from the papers. "I can see that my money has been well taken care of. I am happy that some of the things I brought to your attention have done well also." Cullen nodded. "So that your time will not be tied up," Jacob nodded in return, "I shall be more than happy to translate these documents for my friends." He smiled and stood up to go.

Cullen also stood up and came around the desk to shake hands with each of them. "One last thing," he said as lifted a beautifully wrapped package from behind his desk. "If you would give this to Mac MacTavish, with the gratitude of us all, I would be grateful."

A couple of days later on New Year's Eve, Amos, Jacob and Riley caught the train to Rock River. They gave the drawing Olaf Nordquist had made of them to Mac and his Missus. It was immediately hung among the pictures of the MacTavish family.

At midnight, as the long year of 1878 finally ended, Missus MacTavish, her three adopted " boys", and her very large husband had a sip of the finest scotch money could buy to ring in the new year.

CHAPTER 25

NOTHING TO DO (1879)

January second, 1879, found Amos, Riley and Jacob on the train to Carbon. Amos sat across from Riley and Jacob, with his hat pulled over his eyes, wishing for sleep, even though he had slept well the night before. Usually he would've enjoyed the view out the window, but this time he had too much on his mind.

"Hey, Jacob," Amos spoke from beneath his hat, "what does this whole bunch of paper that Mister Cullen gave me mean?"

Jacob grinned, chuckled slightly and said, "What it means, my dear brother, is that in a few years you will be able to retire and live well. Not that you will be rich, but you will be comfortable. And that goes for you too, Riley. For my own part, I too have made more than enough to live comfortably. I can do what I like to do, and pursue geologic interests for the rest of my life. However, I have no intentions of slowing down yet. As the Children of the Mountain would say, 'Being idle makes you no more than a blade of grass'." He smiled slightly and shrugged.

"So what do you think will happen with this going after Middleton again?" Riley asked. He was looking out the window at the snow as it swirled up around the train.

"I don't know." Amos sounded tired. "I thought going after the bums that beat up on Patches would change things. But it really hasn't; I still get that nightmare once in a while."

"That is because you have not yet finished the task that will ease your mind," Jacob said looking at the floor. "You do not want to accompany them when they go after Middleton, but you know that you will have to go, or you will be haunted for the rest of your life."

The train was just coming into Carbon. Out the window Amos could see the ranch house on the hill east of town. He wished he could just stay on the ranch, but as he got up to get off the train he shrugged his shoulders and sighed. In his heart he knew Jacob was right.

By March, winter had begun to loosen its hold on the Medicine Bow country. Still no word had come from Sam Hanley. The spring roundup got started and there were days that went by when Amos did not even think about Bill Lykins and what was going on at the prison, or what might be coming up. He had twice been to see the Indians in their winter camp at the White Rocks. Each time he had enjoyed himself, and on the second visit he had gotten Jacob to translate for him as he relayed the story of his dreams to the now acting Chief. He could see that being asked for advice brought pride to the Indian leader. There was little more to be said than what Jacob had told him, but for a while it brought him some peace.

The roundup had begun to settle down by June. The ranch had expanded and was now running thousands of cattle. More cowboys had been added, most of whom were related to the men who were already there. A third house was planned to be built along the Medicine Bow River at the north end of Elk Mountain near where the old Overland Stage had crossed the river. The new crew would primarily be responsible for the cattle in the area of Pass Creek. As it turned out the new foreman was to be Mickey O'Malley, the same man that Amos had recovered a knife for when he first came to the TIC. Back then Mickey had been a hard drinking, hard fighting cowhand. As time had gone along he had outgrown it. Now he was about as good a choice as any for the job.

Summer rolled by and on the Fourth of July they had fireworks in the town. The Union Pacific Coal Company had footed the bill for the celebration. Even Amos went with Riley into town and celebrated with a beer at Jim Ross's saloon. They sat in the little stone building and raised their bottles. "Here's to you, Mac," they said as they thought about Mac playing his bagpipes.

Three days later the feeling of anxiousness that Amos had been carrying since Christmas was finally broken by a telegram from Sam Hanley asking that he and Riley come to Laramie in the next week. The message said that horses would be provided when they got to Nebraska. Even so, Amos and Riley decided to take their own to Laramie so they would have something to ride home when they got back.

The next day they loaded their horses and gear on the train and late that afternoon they were in Laramie. They made arrangements at Tom Sherman Senior's livery and then got rooms at the hotel. They stowed their gear and went to see Nathan Tower. Sam Hanley, Bill Lykins, J.L. Smith and of course Nathan were all there. Several more men would join them in North Platte, Nebraska. General Crook had promised a contingency of troops if the outlaws were cornered. They would travel by train to North Platte, Nebraska and then ride north to a place on the Niobrara River that Middleton had named "The Robbers Roost".

"We will be traveling fast and light," Bill Lykins said. "We should arrive at Middleton's cabin at about the same time as the cavalry."

Sam Hanley stood and looked squarely at everyone. "I know there was some question about the actual guilt of some of the men who may have been involved with Middleton before. In this case every single person is to be looked on as the worst sort of criminal, because every one of them is," he said firmly. "They have all ridden with Middleton for several years, and are known to be horse thieves, rustlers, thugs, robbers, and in some cases murderers. You are guaranteed immunity from prosecution for the death of anyone found there. You will shoot first and ask questions later." He emphasized "will" very strongly.

"Will Llewellyn has gone ahead to Grand Island," J. L. Smith said. "He is picking up a man named Hazen, who apparently knew Middleton at one time, to help lead him there. For those of you who may wonder," he looked directly at Amos and Riley, "Smith had his prison time reduced in exchange for a lot of information. I believe his experience there will keep him from ever wanting to commit a crime again." He chuckled coldly. "I'm going to go on ahead to make sure Middleton is where he is supposed to be and keep an eye on him. I have a train to catch boys! I'll join you there in a few days." He rose and went out of the office.

Three days later Sam Hanley, Bill Lykins, Amos and Riley were on the train to North Platte, Nebraska. It was a long train ride, but crossing the prairie brought back memories of his days as a railroad hand and a buffalo hunter. Sadly, there were very few buffalo left. The passing of the great beasts had meant the passing of the plains Indians too. He noticed that the area where he had slept in a tent near Grand Island was already covered up with new buildings. What had once been the "West" was now farmland.

They unloaded their gear and went directly to pick out horses at the stockyard. As usual Amos left that chore up to Riley. Even though tack was to be provided for them, Amos and Riley had too many painful memories of old saddles and Army saddles, so they had brought their own.

There was a pack horse for each two men and they were quickly provisioned with minimal food and shelter. Early the next morning they were headed north. The journey would be about one hundred and twenty miles and they intended to cover it in three to four days. It was the hot season in Nebraska, so they traveled early in the morning and late into the night, and sometimes all night. They relied on a local sheriff, who knew the area well, to guide them.

They made the trip in the allotted time and found J. L. Smith, Will Llewellyn, a man who Amos assumed was Hazen, and a small contingent of cavalry holding several people hostage in a cabin a few miles from the Niobrara River. One of the hostages was Middleton's father-in-law, John Richardson. Cocking his gun, J.L. Smith pointed it at the head of one of the other hostages and said that he would pull the trigger if Richardson refused to lead them to Middleton's hideout. Richardson tearfully agreed to do so, on the promise that his daughter would not be harmed. Smith agreed and soon the whole group was headed for the river.

There was a long shallow canyon containing a small stream leading to the Niobrara River. Richardson said that Middleton and his gang were constructing a camp near the river, but refused to enter the canyon for fear that he would be killed. Two scouts were sent down and soon reported back that perhaps half a dozen men were busy working.

Sam Hanley gathered everyone about him. "We've got them outnumbered badly. However, it concerns me as to where his other men are. There's a good chance they're off somewhere stealing horses and anything else they can get their hands on. I think the best thing we can do is try to surround them quickly and get it over before anyone else comes back."

The soldiers were positioned at high points along the canyon so that anyone trying to ride out could be fired on. The rest of the men fanned out around the camp and, on a signal, attacked. Middleton and five men grabbed their guns and tried to break out. Two men were quickly killed. Lykins and Hazen were still on horse back and charged. Hazen's horse was hit and fell to the ground. Hazen stood but was hit and went down. Lykins rushed to help him, firing his rifle as he went. Middleton was running towards them firing his pistol. Lykins' rifle apparently jammed, for he quickly threw it away, drew his pistol and fired. Middleton was hit in the stomach and staggered away into the brush while the remaining outlaws fled. Lykins got Hazen to cover and tended to his wound. In short order he had Hazen in a wagon headed to a nearby ranch.

Amos, Riley, Sam Hanley and several men stayed behind to look for the wounded Middleton and remaining gang members. Amos had noticed the remains of a caved in trappers' cabin along the stream where he had come in. On a hunch he got Riley and returned to it thinking that one of the escaped men might be hiding there. There were tracks and broken twigs to show that someone had just run through the area. Riley took cover behind some fallen trees and fired at the building. Someone inside fired back and it was obvious that there was just one person. Amos had stayed back out of sight and moved to the back of the building. Inside he could see that whoever it was had only a pistol. Amos leveled his rifle and eased up behind him, then yelled at the top of his lungs, so Riley could hear him, "Drop your gun or I will shoot you!" The outlaw dropped his gun and slowly turned around.

Amos was shocked; in front of him was the spitting image of Jim Baldwin, somewhat thinner and taller, but there was no mistaking who he was.

"Listen Mister," Allen Baldwin sounded very sincere. "We can work something out here. I've got a little money and it's probably more than I'd be worth to you dead. What say I give that to you and you just let me walk out of here?" He reached for a pouch on his belt.

"Do you happen to remember an old meat hunter that you and Newt Simmons beat up on and then stole his horses?" Amos asked. His voice was very deep and angry.

"You mean that old fart over by Centennial?" Baldwin rolled his eyes. "He stunk so bad! I was doing those horses a favor to steal them. Hadn't been for Newt, I would have burned the whole stinkin' damn camp."

Amos was getting madder by the second. "Well, he is a friend of mine, and a better man than you could ever be!" he growled. "You're going to go to prison for what you did. You're damn lucky he's still alive or I would shoot you right here!"

"Just who the hell are you?" Rage was coming into the voice of Allen Baldwin.

"Moss, Amos Moss." the voice was flat and cold. "I'm the man that killed your brother Jim. I'd just as soon kill you too, and if I ever find that son of a bitch Johnny I'll kill him too."

"You're gonna to have to!" Baldwin had spoken his last words. His hand reached behind his back and it came up with a pocket pistol. Amos fired his Winchester and the hollow point bullet destroyed the shoulder of the hand that held the gun. It had not yet hit the floor when a second round hit Baldwin in the chest. The outlaw slumped backwards against the remains of a wall. Amos felt the same rage he had felt when he killed the Union officer who had allowed Toby and Lynette Miller to be murdered. This time he had a gun instead of a rock. Another round followed and another and another, each tearing huge holes, until the rifle was empty. Then both Schofield pistols were emptied. Amos stood gasping for air.

Riley came up and put his arm around Amos. "He's dead now Amos," he said quietly as he squeezed Amos's shoulders. "Who was he?"

162

"That was Allen Baldwin," Amos's voice was still cold and little more than a whisper. "He's the bastard that beat up on Patches."

Riley let go and walked over to the body. He looked for a moment then pulled out one of his Schofields and emptied it. "Come on Amos, I don't think we'll see that nightmare again," he said as he caught Amos's arm.

"We?" Amos asked and looked questioningly at Riley.

Riley looked straight at Amos and said softly, "Yeah, we." he said as he glanced at the bullet riddled body. "Bury him?" Riley asked.

"I only bury what deserves to be buried." Amos's voice was raspy. "That can stay here and rot." They walked away.

They walked back to where the camp had been. The deputies and the soldiers had taken anything of value and had set fire to everything else they could find. Middleton had been found lying in the brush. His wound was not serious but would be painful for a long time. Several members of his gang were dead and he was facing prison time, if not a rope. As J.L. Smith had promised, Richardson's daughter was unharmed, and she was turned over to her father.

A second wagon and team were located and Middleton was tied in it. Bill Lykins had six men guarding the wagon with instructions to shoot the prisoner if they were attacked. In addition he placed a stick of dynamite near Middleton's head. If any of the gang happened to try to rescue their leader they would find nothing left.

After the wagon rolled away, Sam Hanley was the only one of the lawmen still in the camp. He smiled as Amos and Riley walked up. "Well, my friends, it's finally over," He said as he let out a deep sigh. "There's not much left to do here now but leave, and it's a long ride to Laramie."

Made in the USA
Las Vegas, NV
16 September 2022